C F
FENSHAM EL Helicop
Fensham, Elizabeth.
Helicopter man /
MEN 31068236759

WITHDRAWN

WORN,

D0531772

HELICOPTER MAN

HELICOPTER MAN

by
elizabeth
fensham

BLOOMSBURY

Copyright © 2005 by Elizabeth Fensham

All rights reserved. No part of this book may be used or reproduced
in any manner whatsoever without written permission from the publisher,
except in the case of brief quotations embodied in critical articles or reviews.

Published by Bloomsbury Publishing, New York, London, and Berlin
Distributed to the trade by Holtzbrinck Publishers

Library of Congress Cataloging-in-Publication Data
Fensham, Elizabeth.

Helicopter man / Elizabeth Fensham.—1st U.S. ed.
p. cm.
Summary: Peter Sinclair cares for his father, who is mentally ill,
and tries to make the most of their homeless life together.
ISBN-10: 1-58234-981-9 • ISBN-13: 978-1-58234-981-7
[1. Fathers and sons—Fiction. 2. Mental illness—Fiction.
3. Homelessness—Fiction. 4. Australia—Fiction.] I. Title.
PZ7.F3484He 2005   [Fic]—dc22   2004066007

First U.S. Edition 2005
Printed in the U.S.A.
1 3 5 7 9 10 8 6 4 2

Bloomsbury Publishing, Children's Books, U.S.A.
175 Fifth Avenue, New York, NY 10010

All papers used by Bloomsbury Publishing are natural, recyclable products
made from wood grown in well-managed forests. The manufacturing processes
conform to the environmental regulations of the country of origin.

To the brave

P.O. Box 15
McKenzie's Beach
N.S.W. 2955

August 22nd

Dear Pete,

Miss you. What's going on?
Mum has put your pirate mug
on the shelf with Dad's best stuff.
The sea eagles are teaching their
two eaglets to fly. Mum and Dad
say if you ever want to stay, you
can. For as long as you want.

Your Mate,
Vic

PETER SINCLAIR
C/O G.P.O. Melbourne
VICTORIA 3000

(Please forward if possible)

RETURN TO SENDER

1

Diary – Saturday May 6th, Heritage Hotel

a.m. The helicopters are flying low today. Dad has kept us inside.

This morning he said, *Too dangerous to go out, Pete.*

We're both in our sleeping bags.

Dad's trying to think, but he keeps dozing off. His grey hair has fallen out of its ponytail. He's snoring with his mouth open.

I'll organise my pack today in case we have to evacuate.

Sunday May 7th, Heritage Hotel

a.m. So far, so good. Seems to be safe.

Have to be quiet in our nest of sacks up the back here. We're pretty sure no one will find us, though.

The owners have built a brand new garage for their gardening and farm equipment, and their house is away at the end of the garden. This old shed never gets a look-in.

Anyway, it's jammed with stuff. You can hardly squeeze through the door. To get to our cubby, you have to push past a whole lot of broken-down machinery, old chairs, suitcases, a chest of drawers, a mouldy leather bag of golf clubs, boxes of glass jars, a roll of carpet and some wooden tea chests. There are massive cobwebs floating off the ceiling. Dad calls it a circus trapeze because there are dead insects trapped in it, swinging back and forth in the breeze. Coils of rope and wire, lanterns and bits of rusty tools hang like bats from the rafters. The walls and even the fireplace are built out of kerosene tins. Dad says this means it's old. He calls it heritage. Dad reckons it's one of the last original buildings in the area from the time before a lot of this land was cut up into five- and ten-acre blocks. So I've called our shed Heritage Hotel.

There's a window high up on the wall. If I climb on top of some boxes I can see out.

It's sunny. The gold leaves are falling off the trees into mounds of pirates' treasure. I'm busting to get out there and kick them around. Have to wait till tomorrow.

Monday May 8th, Heritage Hotel

a.m. The family from the house have all gone out. Heard two cars take off.

I guess the mum and dad have gone to work and the boy has gone to school. He'd be a couple of years younger than me. I'd say about ten. Don't know where the little girl who has the dummy pinned to her jumper goes to all day.

Stomach hurts. Dad says if the choppers stay away for the afternoon, we'll get out for some food. There are shops up the other side of the valley. Just a General Store that has a petrol bowser out the front, a closed-down butcher's with a To Let sign stuck on the window, a volunteer-run fire station for the bushfire season, and the fish and chip shop. It's a bit spooky how those buildings sit sort of in the middle of nowhere surrounded by a bit of forest and a few orchards and farms. To get to them from here, you go down through the sheep paddock, over the wire of the back fence, slish-slosh through the marshy bit, and up through the reserve which is full of mountain ash, long grass and blackberries that catch and rip your legs and arms like millions of little fish hooks.

There are two things I like about the store. On a warm day you can sit out on the big verandah sipping a cool drink. Second thing, when you walk inside, the fly-screen door goes thwack and makes a little bell tinkle. I like the sound of that bell. But the wood outside needs a paint and the old bloke who runs the store is a bit of a freak. Why would you bother having a shop if you can't stand anyone asking to buy something? His shelves are half empty and I'll never again buy another one of his weird-tasting ice creams with their soft cones. Dad calls him 'cranky'. It could be because he spends most of his day in that tiny room he has off to one side. I keep wanting to see behind the curtain in the doorway. He's always got the races on the radio – the dogs or the horses. I've decided to call him Dog Breath.

The Asian fish and chip man is good to us. Every time we go he gives us an extra-big serve of chips and usually a couple of potato cakes for free. He bows when he hands them to us.

A specially for little fella, he says. *Make him very big man.*

I like the way Dad bows back.

Dad's got good manners.

Tuesday May 9th, Heritage Hotel

Didn't make it to the fish and chip shop yesterday. Helicopters.

Today another helicopter. Snooping round the hills. Sometimes diving along a gully. *Like a hawk after a sparrow* is the way Dad puts it. When they are close, Dad freaks. He crawls into the corner and puts his hands over his ears. He's gone to sleep again. It's better for him like that.

Rations low. Just stale bread. No way will Dad give me money to go to the shops on my own.

Can't hack this. Have to eat something. Keep thinking about the General Store. It'd be a sure bet after closing time.

Evening – 8.30

Got back about half an hour ago. Shoulder hurting.

Dad's been going off his head at me. Bad. Well, as off your head as you can when you're hiding and you can't shout. He'd heard the shotgun. A noise like that echoes up and down the valley. The blood just below my shoulder really scared him. Didn't notice it till he did. With the blood cleaned off you can see it's two little holes about a thumbnail apart. Shotgun pellets.

My plan was simple enough. Dad was deep, deep asleep late afternoon when I snuck out the door of our shed with my backpack on. It's so good to get outside. Days and days of living amongst other people's junk and hiding from helicopters. Took Dad's usual route through the sheep paddock and down to the marshy creek. Lost my runner in the mud. Got a twig and fished it out. Squelched my way up through the forest. On my own is kind of different to walking with Dad. Barely any sunlight. Those trees are close together and at least two hundred feet straight up. Dad says they used to be logged for ships' masts.

Near the top of the valley, decided to hurdle that giant fallen log that Dad and I usually take a breather on. Started running to get powered up, but mid-leap decided to land on, not over the log. Looked down the other side and there's this almighty big six-foot brown snake all coiled up having a snooze. Did a detour. Came out of the trees pretty close to where the shops are.

Hard to believe all this was roughly two hours ago. About six o'clock it was already getting dark. I was going to do a 'break in and borrow' after Dog Breath had closed up the General Store and left for the night. Five o'clock is as late as he ever stays open.

There was a bit of a moon. Only the fish and chip shop was lit up. I stepped out on to the road and walked to the store. Never noticed before tonight how much those wooden steps and verandah floorboards creak. Tested out two windows at the front. Locked. Had more luck with the window down the side. There was a broken pane.

Worked my hand in and up to the swivel lock. Freed it and slid the window up slow and gentle, but the old wood kind of groaned. Next I got my leg through the window and then the rest of me was inside.

Knew where I was heading – to the shelf with the jams and then the bread rack and after that, well, anything that I liked the look of. Slipped a small jar of jam into my pants' pocket. Am just about to take off my backpack for the serious work when Dog Breath pushes through the curtain from the side room. He's yelling, *You're dead meat! You're dead meat!* And there he is in his old man's underpants and his floppy chest and wiry whiskers. He's so white he's almost glow-in-the-dark. But worst of all, he's waving a double-barrelled shotgun around.

Should have known a cranky old bloke like that would have no home to go to. Have my hands in the air, but Dog Breath is saying, *I'll teach ya not to do this again! Face the wall and take off that pack!* I'm not sure what he plans to do with me, but sure as hell I'm not going to wait and find out. I've got this picture of Dog Breath just burying me in a hole somewhere in the bush behind his store and Dad never knowing where I'd gone.

Start taking off my pack and sliding towards the open window. Dog Breath keeps moving the gun as

I move. *Stand still, maggot!* Dog Breath's saggy arms are shaking. He has the gun held at his waist, but it's wobbling all over the place. It's now or never. My backpack is off and I chuck it straight at Dog Breath's head and run for the window. Bang! There's a gaping great hole in the wall plaster just to the right of my shoulder.

I'm out that window, along the side verandah and heading down the backyard. Funny how you think quick at times like these. I have it figured out that if I do a zigzag I might just stay clear. So there I am running for a line of scrub at the bottom of the paddock behind the shop. Running like I've got fire coming out of my backside. And then all hell breaks loose, like stepping on a landmine.

A dog, a big one with square jaws and a muscly body, is coming at me. Little glass eyes full of hate. It's black with light brown stripes that gleam in the moonlight – sort of like a Tasmanian tiger or a hyena. I remember reading once that you shouldn't run when a dog is about to attack. I'm frozen to the spot anyway. But it's not slowing the dog down. Red eyes, mouth wide open, slobber flying, teeth and jaws that could pull a pony down.

Standing still isn't working. Am just about to try punching the dog in the snout like I've heard you should do with sharks. The dog hurls itself at my face, but its head jerks back with a snap. It's chained to a tree near its kennel. Bang! The gun again. I hear the dog yelp and a sound like rain on leaves. I'm running straight for the scrub and commando-rolling into it.

Must have run in a low crouch through that scrub for about ten minutes. Have to keep the road in view over to my left. Am a bend away from the store before I sneak out on to the road. No one. Race across to the forest on the other side. It's too dark in there to run, but I'm heading home like a well-trained pigeon when CRASH, something big is stomping through the bush behind me. I press my face and hands against the rough trunk of a mountain ash. Tall and strong. Like hugging Dad. And I remember Dad telling me the American Indians used to hug trees to give them courage before battle.

The crashing is coming nearer. I pick a branch off the ground. Straight and about the length of a spear. There's this thudding and twigs cracking. Getting closer. I raise my branch ready to clobber whoever is coming for me. The enemy comes into view. He's a short heavy fellow. Dark fur. A black swamp wallaby. Thank God.

Damn. Torch is fading. Needs new batteries.

Wednesday May 10th, Heritage Hotel

Shoulder okay this morning.

Yesterday was some day. The only way I could stop Dad telling me off and going on and on about leaving the shed without letting him know was by handing him the strawberry jam I'd brought back. Was lucky it stayed in my pocket. Told Dad I found it on my walk. Sort of true. He's so starving he stopped and said, *Good on you, Pete*, then wrenched the lid off the jar. We finished the jam on bread this morning. Both of us have slept most of the afternoon. Ate the last two slices of bread when we woke about an hour ago.

Am still so hungry. Usually this diary keeps me going. Feeling too tired to write any longer.

Thursday May 11th, Heritage Hotel

A good day. No helicopters. Dad said we could get out.

Left mid-morning. Walked up to bus stop near fish and chip shop. Scared shitless Dog Breath might be about. Stuck close to Dad's side and kept the hood of my jacket pulled right down over my eyes. Caught bus down out of the hills to suburbs and went to Social Security. Those retards behind the counter treat you like dirt.

Dad went to Melbourne Uni. Dad's quiet and polite. When the losers behind the counter are rude, I can tell Dad's getting pissed off by the way his back gets stiffer and he stands taller. He's a big man, my dad – a bit over six feet. But I wish his clothes weren't so crumply.

Just as well Dad was there today.

There was this family with lots of quiet sad-looking kids and what I guess was the wife and grandma who were covered up in long shirts and scarves. Everyone was staring at them. Standing behind the counter, one of these morons wearing a Mickey Mouse tie started making trouble. He was gabbling at the father who couldn't understand much English.

Please slow, said the father. *Please slow.*

But would Mr White Collar and Tie slow down? No way.

The father started crying. The social security guy just shoved the paperwork at him and told him to find a friend who could speak English. So this is where Dad steps in.

I was sent to help you, Dad says to the crying man. He probably only understood the word *help*. And Dad has a kind voice, too. That would come across to anyone. Dad takes the paperwork and sits down with the family. Twenty minutes later their form is filled in. Next, I'm getting my head patted by the women and they give me these lollies to eat. Dad says they're refugees from Afghanistan. Dad wants to know how much justice these people are going to get here.

Went to the Summerville shopping complex. Dad says we're safe there.

Saw a magic show (for the little kids, but still good). The magician made a dove come out of a silk hanky. He stuck the dove into a tiny box and pulled out a giant white duck with a diamond collar round its neck. Next he disappeared the duck. After that he borrowed a fifty-dollar note from a mum and made it disappear. Then he magicked the duck back and the fifty-dollar note was tucked inside its collar.

Visited the complex's Community Drop-in Centre. Bit of a fancy name for just a room on level three wedged between Tattoo Haven and Guys and Dolls Hair Salon. Free coffee and biscuits for Dad. Free Milo for me.

Went to the Myer toy department. Played on the Super Nintendo with a blotchy kid who was off school because he was getting over chickenpox. He had two poxy scars. One next to his eye and one on his back which he was pretty proud of.

He pulled up his T-shirt to show me.

Feeling tired. Will finish this tomorrow.

Friday May 12th, Heritage Hotel

Yesterday was good. Also did a bit of mouse research on the Internet at the shopping complex's library. Mouse pregnancies last only twenty-one days and they can have over twenty babies at a time. Eight to twelve is average.

Am getting to be pretty much of an expert on mice. We live with a city of them. Dad says they're worst in autumn. They are escaping into here from the cold that's coming. They're not shy. They just hurry and climb and plop all over the place. But those cartoons about mice lie. They don't seem to like cheese. I've left some out and they haven't touched it. Their favourite hobby is pooing everywhere. Even in my sleeping bag. It makes a kind of thick smell.

I'd hate being a mouse, but I wouldn't mind being an echidna. Also found out on the Internet yesterday (got a bit sidetracked by mating information) that an echidna male has two heads to its penis. When I told Dad, he asked if that meant you'd get into trouble for two-timing.

21

Things we bought yesterday:
Socks from the charity shop.
A book for Dad and two books for me (also from the charity shop). One is about these kids who survive an invasion of Australia. They know all about hiding, too. And a fantastic one called *One Hundred Mighty Mouse Facts*.
A plastic bucket with lid. Forget all that sneaking outside with a trowel and paper.
Batteries for torch.
Some tins of sweetened condensed milk, small jar of Vegemite, fruit, cheese in foil, bread, margarine, tins of fish and a bottle of cordial with 40% real fruit juice.

What we ate:
Lots of hot food samples from the sales ladies in the supermarket.
Take-away roast lamb and vegetables from the food court. Yum.
Raspberry ice cream in a waffle cone. Double yum.

Have spent most of today reading and eating.

Saturday May 13th, Heritage Hotel

The boy's name is Neville. It's an easy name to yell. His mother shrieks it a lot during violin practice.

The music room is the closest one to our shed. Every night, here we go! Mother plays the piano and Neville scratches on the gut. That's what the strings used to be made of.

Neville starts with about a billion rhythm variations on *Twinkle Twinkle Little Star*, e.g. twinkle twinkle, twinkle twinkle, little, little star, star etc. (Dad and I went to sleep last night humming *Twinkle*. This morning we made a pact never again to let that tune pass our lips.) Neville is pretty good on the Twinkles, but when the music gets harder the show really begins.

Neville starts whingeing. I swear his whinge is higher pitched than his violin playing. It makes you want to smash something. That's probably what he wants his mum to do. Anything to get her off his back. But the mum takes a long time to break.

She begins all loud and cheerful. *That's D flat, not D sharp, dear. Hold your fingers properly. No slumping, now. That's it, back straight. Come on, Neville, you can't hold the bow like a hacksaw.*

After that, they both crack. Neville makes a wild sound on his violin. His mother starts ranting and raving. Neville keeps scratching away on his violin. Then I bet he must chuck the violin down and he runs outside. (The first time he did that, I was scared he'd make for this place. But I think he's spooked by it. I'd be, too, if I didn't have Dad.)

His mother comes out on the back verandah.

N E V I L L E! she screams. *You can stay out there with the cat.*

And that's what he does. He has a favourite bush near the shed that he climbs into with his cat and he says, *Stuff Mum! Stuff violin!*

Neville's winning. Yesterday, he only practised for five minutes.

Dad says we'll move soon as he thinks it's safe. I'm ready.

Had a fright late last night. Thought we'd been found. We were in our sleeping bags just nodding off. There was this terrible thumping across the roof. I go stiff and still.

Then I feel Dad's strong arm around me.

Possums with gumboots on, he says.

We both start chuckling in the dark. That was one of Mum's jokes. Then Dad goes all serious. *They took her, but they're not getting us.*

2

Sunday May 14th, Heritage Hotel

Have been thinking about Mum today. If she'd wanted me to learn the violin, I'd have learnt it. We could have done the pubs together. I'd play. She'd sing.

It's Mum's singing I remember best. Every bedtime she used to sing, *Lulla by, by, you've got the moon to dream on*. She'd be sitting up in bed next to me, trying to sing me to sleep. Most times she'd be asleep before I was. And when she and Dad were doing the dishes she'd sing, *Black, black is the colour of my true love's hair*. That was Dad's favourite, even though his hair used to be light brown.

Mum was the one with the black hair. It was long and thick with a reddishness mixed in with the dark. Can't remember her face. When my photo of her was stolen, I went ballistic. Feeling ballistic now, just thinking about that.

Dad says I look like Mum – blackish hair and lots of it, same shaped face and eyes except they are cloud-blue like Dad's (not deep brown like Mum's). On Thursday, in the shopping mall toilets, I stared in the mirror and said, *Hello, Pete*, but the voice was all wrong. Thought I might cry. Wanted to bash my hand right through that mirror and get to Mum on the other side. Miss her all the time. Seriously all the time. Can't let on to Dad, though. He gets all worked up. Sometimes I feel like I've skipped being a kid and just gone on to being old.

Action list for today:
Read more of my book.
Make a no-harm mouse trap.
Look in some of those boxes.
Draw a mouse city.
Get outside for a while before the others get up.
Do some work in my Language book.
Do some maths. HELP!

Dad's feeling uptight today. He doesn't like to worry me.

All he'll say is, *I'm here to keep you safe. I need some time to myself to seek guidance.*

I know not to bother him.

Wish he'd tell me why we're running.

Monday May 15th, Heritage Hotel

Hate weekends. Had to be so careful yesterday.

The whole family were out there in the paddock.

Dad read me some of *The Hobbit* yesterday afternoon. It must be the third time we've read it together.

Dad does these excellent voices. Especially for Gollum and Smaug. He makes up the tunes for the dwarf and goblin songs, too. The copy we've got is the best you can get with the colour illustrations Tolkien did himself. It's got 'Parkdale Library' stamped on the inside cover and at the back. Dad says we'll return it when we're back in the area.

Made a mouse trap out of a four-litre ice-cream container. I've leant a piece of balsa wood like a ladder against the edge with a bit of biscuit on the top. If I can get a mouse to run up the plank it will tip into the box.

My career choices update:
Writer
Archaeologist
Millionaire
Vet
Magician

Tuesday May 16th, Heritage Hotel

Dear Mum,

I know you'll never be able to read this, but writing to you like you're still around makes me feel better.

I'm exhausted. Just how long do we have to keep going like this? I know Dad needs me, but my head hurts from doing so much worrying and thinking. Was that why you used to sometimes go off by yourself and cry?

That time I took you the dandelion and said, *Please don't be sad, Mum*, you said, *I'm just a bit tired.* I kind of knew you weren't just tired. And another time I found you crying, you said, *I'm sad for Daddy because he's lost his job again.* I'd got used to that. The job in the council gardens. The paint factory job. The assistant chef in the cafe. And the big job, the one Dad was so rapt about, as a journalist for the local newspaper. Were you worrying and worrying and thinking and thinking, too?

When we got off the bus and were walking home from the shopping complex the other day, a car went past – a family driving home in their comfortable car. No wind creeping down the back of your coat collar. No water squelching up the cracks in your runners. And quick. A trip that took us a day must take them just an hour or two. One day,

Dad and I will have a car and our own home.

When we're down in the suburbs, I like looking over the fences into people's windows just on teatime. The mums, dads and kids are strolling about doing ordinary family things. It looks safe and golden warm, like lounging with your feet up by an open fire. That'll be us as soon as possible.

Storm last night. The tin on the roof crashed and made tearing sounds like someone ripping open a cardboard box. A billion leaks. The bottom of my sleeping bag got soaked. The floor boards are gappy. The wind came through and made my back cold.

Was missing you extra badly. Had a bit of a cry. I didn't want to upset Dad. I usually can stop myself. But not this time. Dad took me in his arms and we stayed curled up together the rest of the night. Got a sore throat today. Feeling *mouldy* like you used to call it.

I do a lot of thinking about the time you went. Was it back then that our troubles started?

Love from,

Pete

P.S. I tie your green hair ribbon round my wrist every night before I sleep.

P.P.S. Have just discovered a grey mouse in my ice-cream container. It's got tiny bright black eyes. I reckon it's thinking clever thoughts.

Wednesday May 17th, Heritage Hotel

Neville and co. have gone off for the day. Rain has stopped. Feeling like I have a razor blade wedged in my throat and a couple of knives through my back. Dad's given me some vitamin C.

Sleeping bags are drying in the sun. Am sitting on a box leaning against the trunk of a big old tree. Dad says, *Why don't you give the writing a rest?* Have just told him, *Can't.* He says, *What you got in there?* I say, *Nothing much.* Dad just says, *Could be dangerous if they get hold of that.* Scares me to think of not having my book. I like writing down the good stuff and I kind of need to get the bad stuff down. It's a film in my head that won't turn off unless I can tell my story. Couldn't keep going without this. *Just want to be a writer like you used to be*, I say. It's the truth, but not the main reason. Dad has just nodded. He's off my back.

Dad's restless. He doesn't laugh as much. Keeps searching through his books for information he needs. Won't tell me much more than that. His eyes are all wide with lots of white showing – like that horse looked in the yard at the abattoir a couple of years back.

Thursday May 18th, Heritage Hotel

Small plane flew over this morning. Dad won't let me out.

Been thinking about McKenzie's Beach. We were safe up there in New South Wales for almost a whole year. Our cottage burrowed like a wombat into the scrub on the clifftop. Dad was always saying, *This has a view like you'd get from a ship's crow's-nest!*

It was sunnier there. Considering Dad can't swim, it was good of him to let me go in the water. That first week he'd watch for hours and only call me if I went out too far. Once I had Vic to swim with, Dad didn't seem to worry any more. Just left us to it. I remember nearly living in the sea. We were only nine, too.

Even grey days were good. Dad and I would sit and look out the window. We'd look at the waves with their white tips rolling to for ever. Sometimes we put on our coats and walked along the beach with our heads pressing into the wind.

Dad taught me to play Scrabble in that cottage. I'd cheat and Dad would act like he didn't know. We'd always play at night. You could hear the ocean thumping against cliffs and crushing shells on the beach.

It was good the way friends used to drop in.

Like Tom Longhorn when he felt like a yarn. His hair was that thick and white. And his face had lines as deep as ditches. You could've stuck your finger in one. Tom told the tallest fishy tales you've ever heard. Whoppers. But the locals still reckon he's one of the best fishermen up or down the coast.

And the De Lucia family. How they'd walk up to our place from their cottage on the beach if Anna wanted a break from her painting or Marco from his pottery. Dad would make herb tea for Anna and Marco and iced chocolate for Vic and me. He and I would scoff our drinks then nick outside to muck around.

Vic's a true expert on just about anything you want to know – swimming, cricket, wildlife and birds, rocks and shells, how to make spears, how to spit for a metre and three quarters, how to whistle with no fingers in your mouth and heaps more.

Was fun when it was our turn to visit the De Lucias and having to eat and drink with all Marco's sea-theme stuff like shell-shaped bowls, and cups with mermaids for handles. Embarrassing if your fingers touched the boobs, but.

I reckon Victor is happy being their only child. Vic's special. Anna got pregnant when she was 42 years old and she thought she couldn't. Victor is short for victory.

Asked Dad if Peter meant petrified. Dad said I was close. Peter comes from an ancient Greek word meaning rock. I like that.

I've called my mouse Mervin. Uncle Mervin was a relative of Dad's. He was 20 years old when he died fighting the Germans in Greece during the Second World War. Dad says it's considerate of me to carry on Mervin's name, because he didn't have any kids. Mervin the Second has good fighting instincts, too. When I was feeding him some bread, he bit me.

Dad's barricaded the door with some tea chests.

3

Friday May 19th, Heritage Hotel

Vic, you're the best friend I've ever had. To be honest, you're just about the only friend I've had, not counting Matthew O'Neil back in grade one and a few kids I've met at McDonald's or on buses and at train stations round New South Wales and Victoria.

Could do with hearing what you'd say about everything going on here. You'd probably say, *Stuff this for a joke. Let's go AWOL.* Trouble is, I have to stick with Dad. I'm the only one who can help. He's gone right into himself. His eyes are getting all starey. A few minutes back I asked, *Remember when Vic and me caught that whopping great tuna with a hand-line?* And he said in this not-there way, *Good idea.*

Saturday May 20th, Heritage Hotel

Today was thinking about your birthday, Vic. It's May. Now you're twelve. The six-week difference is over. You've caught up with me again. Wonder whether you look the same as the last time I saw you when we were ten. I'm getting a bit of hair under my armpits and down below. Thought that only happened when you turned thirteen. You'd be able to tell me. I could talk to you about anything.

Yeah. We could talk, all right. And we liked all the same things. Mum used to say you shouldn't like people just because they do what you want, but it was different for you and me. Sort of like our thoughts connected.

We stuck out. Your home-made clothes with parrot pictures all over them. As always, my second-hand stuff. With our dark hair, tanned skin and definitely not-cool clothes we must have looked like we'd run away from the circus. Other kids in the area were already wearing brand-name shorts and T-shirts. They used to call you Polly 'cos of those parrots. I asked you once, *Doesn't it piss you off?* and you spat one of your champion metre and three quarter spits and said, *Couldn't give a rat's arse.*

Our parents were different from most of the grown-ups at McKenzie's. Looked different and were different. It wasn't just that your folks were artists and Dad wrote poetry, but Anna being a vegan, Marco belonging to Greenpeace, and Dad with his hatred for the government meant some of the locals treated Dad and your folks like they were useless hippies.

I'll always remember the first time we saw you lot on the beach. There was this short, blue-eyed man with dark hair that was so curly it looked like it was in knots. He was wearing a sarong and teaching this curly-haired kid dressed in a parrot shirt and parrot shorts to juggle apples and oranges. And there was this tall lady with long goldy-coloured hair and a falling-apart straw hat on her head. She was sitting on a folding stool with a pencil and pad, sketching you both. Dad and I were just standing and watching and you came across with your fruit and said, *Want a try?*

Out of all the schools I've been to, home-schooling at your place was definitely the best. Working round that gi-normous wooden table in the front room. Pot-belly stove blazing away when it was cold. Glass verandah doors wide open on hot days so you could see the sand dunes and the ocean.

PE – Swim, walk, play cricket or canoe on lagoon.

Music – Become a Pavarotti expert by hearing Marco in his pottery room singing along with his *Three Tenors* CD.

Maths – Do basics, but not too much 'cos none of the grown-ups liked it either.

History and geography – Listen to the weird/scary/funny stories Anna and Marco told about the three years they travelled the world after they left college.

Look at all those travel books in your bookcase.

Join in the deep and meaningfuls your mum and dad used to have with Dad about the environment and Aboriginal land rights and stuff.

Art – Didn't have to go to Paris for this, did we? I liked the way Marco and Anna couldn't give a stuff about us making a mess if you and I decided to get creative. Hope you're all using the mug I made with the skull and crossbones decoration.

Literature – Read whatever we want for as long as we want.

Creative writing – You've got to admit, Dad was a cool teacher. He made us feel good about what we wrote because he got all wrapped up in it. Remember him saying about 'Black Knight's Revenge', *Let's make a film of this!* and we did?

I still tell Dad he should give teaching a try. I ask him to do the course or whatever it is to be a teacher. He says that one day he might when the time's right. When's that?

Sunday May 21st, Heritage Hotel

The good thing about home-schooling is that you usually get through your work quicker.

Any time summer or winter, I can see us down at the beach or exploring the rocks.

I'm thinking about our favourite summer rock pool, shaped like a bath and always warm from the sun. We'd be sitting there talking for ages.

That was an awesome cave you showed me. Big enough for a gang of pirates to live in. And sort of secret. Only idiots like you and me would risk getting to it. A few times I jumped that metre-wide canyon of water – all black and swirling – and wondered if I'd make it.

Have forgotten the name of the next beach that you can get to at low tide from round the rocks. It has that lagoon with pelicans and black swans. I really liked those times Tom Longhorn would let us go with him searching for sand-worms on the lagoon flats at sunset. I remember dragging our sacks around in the sea spray – Tom called it spindrift – and watching how the water on the lagoon would turn all pink. We practised our life-saving in there, too. It was nice of Tom to give us those lessons.

You are definitely the best farter I've ever known.

You could fart whenever you wanted. You played it like a French horn. Wish I still had that list we made of fart words. I've been trying to remember the fifteen, but I can only think of eleven:

Pop off
A ripper
S.B.D. (silent but deadly)
Sub woofa
Bum burp
Gas
Methane
Farp
Loud and proud
Foofie
Thunder Down Under

I've decided Mervin must be lonely. Have made him as comfy as possible – soft grass to lie on, a jar lid with water, bread and fruit. But he spends a lot of time trying to scrabble up the sides of his box and the water keeps getting knocked over. I've made another mouse trap out of a big tin. Mervin needs a wife.

Monday May 22nd, Heritage Hotel

Dad must have written over twenty poems that year. Remember how your mum and dad wanted him to put the best ones in competitions? Dad was too humble or something. Anyway, he never did send any off. Now there's only one poem left. I read it almost every day. I'm going to make a copy in my book this afternoon. Might even send it off to the *Big Issue*.

The Children

The dying embers of a summer day,
And the children call to each other and begin
To come up from the valley of the sea.
They move as if in dream and driftingly
Climb the slow steep dunes of drifting sand
Where harsh sea grasses grow and the slopes
    beyond
Of stones and hunch-back scrub that climb
    towards
The summit cottages where windows burn
With smouldering eastern fire.

Farther and faintlier still their voices call,
Till cottage panes forget an eastern fire
And turn to lamplight.

Why is it that even when you try really hard to think positively, sad bits push themselves through like the cold air that right now is coming under a crack in the shed door?

This poem is the only bit of McKenzie's I still have. That's you and me, Vic, the kids who run back to your place at the end of a day on the beach.

I truly reckon Dad's as good as Shakespeare. It helps to remember. It gets me away from the troubles. But it also reminds me that something terrible happened to the rest of those poems.

Heard a bumping noise in the shed last night. It turned out to be Mervin's future wife – or maybe his brother – escaping from my trap. I got a peek at her/him running for cover.

Tuesday May 23rd, Heritage Hotel

Today I've been thinking back to that first helicopter. And how bad I feel about never being able to explain to you, Vic. I think about it lots. Over and over. Maybe one day I'll get to show you this and you might understand.

We'd been moving around a lot for a couple of years, but at McKenzie's it felt like Dad and I might stay. Then one Saturday afternoon, late, Tom Longhorn drops by with some whiting. He's caught them off the rocks. Like always, he says, *G'day mate. Hooked more than enough for the wife and me.* He smiles and his face goes all wrinkly. He puts the soggy newspaper parcel on our bench. Dad thanks him and shakes his hand. I'm happy Dad has Tom for a friend. Dad has been a bit sad or something over the last few days. I watch Tom walk back down the hill in his blue singlet and shorts. *Can I fish with you tomorrow?* I call out. *If they're still running, mate*, he calls back.

Dad grills the fish for tea. We've just sat down at the table. *May the Lord make us truly grateful*, says Dad. I'm thinking the Lord didn't have to try with me. I'm grateful. I love our place. Am sitting in my favourite chair, looking out to sea. The breeze has got stronger this afternoon and the blue curtains are flapping. There's the sound of the sea and the sound of the curtains flapping and that's all.

All of a sudden, I can hear a motor noise. Next, this roar like a monster lawnmower comes towards our side of the hill. Dad gets that terrified look. *They've found us*, he whispers. He pulls me under the table. I look up at the window and see a helicopter heading straight for our house. The tea trees outside are lashing about like some hurricane has hit. Then the helicopter takes off low and slow over the sea.

We stay under the table till it's dark, then Dad makes me pack. He locks the doors and windows and pulls the curtains shut. He won't have the lights on. Packing in the dark and in a hurry is hard. I miss a few things. It's worrying me that you, Vic, are waiting down on the beach. We've spent the day making that massive big bonfire out of driftwood. We're going to light it tonight.

When there's a knock on the door, I know it's you. Then you call out, *Y'there, Pete?* Dad pulls me close to him and puts his finger on my lips. I don't yell back. You knock some more. *Come on out and stop tricking.* I can hear you walking round the house and trying to look in the windows. Then you leave. In my head I'm shouting, *Don't go, Vic!*

Dad wouldn't even let me leave a letter for you. He said it might be found and used as evidence.
Sorry, Vic.

4

Wednesday May 24th, Heritage Hotel

Success. Heard a scrabbling in my trap just now. Found this very small mouse in there. She's also grey. Asked Dad for a good name. He says we might as well keep it in the family. He suggests Meredith. That was Mum's mother's name. She died over in England when Mum was really little. Nobody would mind us using the name considering Granddad died when I was two.

Mervin and Merrie are getting along okay, but they waste a lot of time rushing round the ice-cream container trying to get out.

The barricade is a dumb idea. It takes Dad ten minutes to pull it apart to let me out for a leak. I could use our bucket, but that's for nights. A leak's my only excuse to get outside in daytime. Am trying to figure out the danger. Could help if I knew.

It's a jigsaw puzzle. With a couple of pieces missing. Have been setting the pieces out. The three of us – Mum, Dad and me – are there at home. Six whole years ago. Living in our little yellow house we rented at Willow Hill, out on the northern edge of Melbourne. There's Dad's vegie garden, Mum's flowers and herbs, the chooks, and Marmalade, the cat. And there's Mum's good friend – old, bald, nearly blind Miss Weiss who's over the fence. If I'm not too freaked out to walk through her cactus jungle, I can visit her for home-made ginger biscuits. There's the singing memories. And the tickle fights – Dad tickling Mum and me on their big bed. We're all laughing.

But there's the night I get woken up by the spookiest crashing noises. I creep out of bed and follow the noises to the front hall. There's Mum chucking wire coat hangers. Just chucking coat hangers as hard and far as she can down the hallway. And Dad's standing there, totally quiet, looking like he doesn't know what to do.

Thinking back to those times makes me wonder if it's all been Dad's fault? I'm scared to ask. Dad's all I've got.

Have spent most of the day reading and drawing. Dad's gone into himself. He hardly speaks. Am dead sick of this place.

Thursday May 25th, Heritage Hotel

Dad reckons Merv and Merrie are too smelly to live with. Told him if he wants one of the cleanest creatures on earth as a pet then he'd better get ready for an ice-cream container of cockroaches. They really are one of the cleanest creatures. That's a fact.

Cockroaches get me thinking of Room 19. Dad reckons that accommodation house down the end of Flinder's Street should have been shut down. Me, too. But it was somewhere to go after getting back to Melbourne from McKenzie's. Sometimes I dream about Room 19 and the gi-normous cock-roaches in the beds, the basin and up the walls. I can see my footprints in the grey carpet that's so full of dust and fleas you'd never believe it was supposed to be brown. And I run to the one little window, but all you can see is a brick wall of some other building. You could almost touch it if you leaned out far enough.

Those first days back were murder.

Spring up on the New South Wales coast and spring in Melbourne are two different things. You couldn't hack it, Vic. It was that wet and cold. The people looked white and sniffly. I kept asking Dad to take me back to you guys. But I got used to it. We were stuck with Room 19 for only a few weeks, anyway. After that we started our shifting around the city and around Victoria again. Like usual.

Friday May 26th, Heritage Hotel

It's dark in here, Vic. Can only just see to write, even with the torch lying next to me.

Really, really want to be out of this shed and down in the city.

That first day back in Melbourne from McKenzie's wasn't just wet, it was freezing. The weather people said it was snowing in the hills. Dad and I headed straight for the National Art Gallery – flash toilets and warm. We've been to the gallery that many times, reckon I could give a guided tour of the section with the old Australian paintings. I like the ones that tell a story.

But there's one picture I hate. Usually, I walk straight past it, but this day I couldn't help myself looking at it. It's made of three different paintings side by side. Massive. Each bit tells a part of the story.

The first painting shows this pioneer man with his wife out in the bush. They're on their own and you can tell life's tough. She's sitting down with her head in her hands, like she's had about enough.

The next painting shows all the hard work, the forest cleared a bit and a hut with smoke coming out the chimney. The husband is sitting on a log and the wife is holding a baby who has his little chubby arm round her neck. The third painting is what I can't handle, 'cos it's the same place (except the forest has been cleared even more so you can see a faraway city which I guess is Melbourne) and the husband is kneeling looking at a cross and you know the wife died and probably the kid.

What really gets to me is that for some people, no matter how hard they try, life just gets worse and worse.

Apart from the gallery, we have our network – just like everywhere else we go. If it's a feed you need, there's a few places you can get food vouchers or a sit-down meal. One of the best feeds is at the Burke Street Baptist church. We're regulars. Dad says he likes the friendly family atmosphere. Friendly? Yeah. Family? Not. Anyway, that's where we went after the gallery on our first day.

When we walked in, Carmen (she lives upstairs and helps with the meals) came running over and hugged me. She gave me an extra-big serving of everything and sat at our table.

Where've you been, Pete? It's been more than a year. Dad sent me a *Keep your mouth shut* look and I said, *Just around.*

Dad relaxed a bit after stowing away his Irish

stew and banana custard. Carmen and Dad got into a rave about the end of the world. She didn't agree with Dad that it would be coming soon.

She said, *Come on, Michael. I know our planet has some serious problems, but what if I got run over by a bus this afternoon?* She reckoned that would be the end of the world for her, so that all she cares about is that today she is kind and caring to her friends and family and even people who aren't her friends. She said, *No need to get our knickers in a knot. It'll be curtains for every one of us at some point.*

That's what Carmen said.

She said it nicely, so Dad didn't mind. Dad even joked. He said Carmen was getting her metafores mixed. Don't know what a metafore is, but it must have been a good joke 'cos Carmen laughed her head off.

Carmen and Dad get along well.

But if it's a real heart-to-heart talk I need, I look out for my old Aboriginal mate, Uncle Jack. Not sure whether that's because he's old or because he's Koorie. Maybe both. I like the way when he comes down from the bush to visit his city relatives, he still has time for others. Uncle Jack spends hours socialising on the streets.

Uncle Jack's favourite spot is sitting outside the cathedral. Everyone knows him. He's pretty black and one of his front teeth is missing. You get to notice that 'cos he laughs a lot. Sure, he drinks a bit too much, but he won't take any cheek from the kids who hang around there. He hates drugs and really hates dealers. He bashes up the dealers. Anyone but them looks up to him. He makes you feel you belong even though there's no exact place you can call home.

Saturday May 27th, Heritage Hotel

Wouldn't admit it to Dad, but Merv and Merrie do stink. Dad and I probably stink a bit, too, but we're used to ourselves. Usually Dad can't stand going without a shower for too long. Am missing our once-a-week shower at Traveller's Aid.

I've got to give it to him, Dad tries. Sometimes he can be pretty strict. Like that second day back in Melbourne from McKenzie's. That day we shower and start off clean, have a late breakfast at Maccas and then take in the free pictures – it's *Star Wars* – at the Salvation Army Headquarters. After that, we drop in at the cathedral for a food hamper. The St Paul's people like Dad. William who works there says to Dad, *How's the lad going with his school-work?* And Dad says, *He'll be going to Oxford.* And I'm thinking, *Yeah, right.*

By then it's time for the choirboys. Those poor guys have to sing in the cathedral every single afternoon.

They're a sad-looking bunch. So would I be if I had to dress up in those frills each day. When they sing it gets me thinking too much about heaven and Mum. Dad must think this, too, 'cos he walks out quickly.

We cross the road to Young and Jackson's. Dad tells me to wait outside. He's only going to have one beer. But it must be more than one beer he has. He's gone that long. If I had some money of my own, I could do a bit of shopping. I get thinking of this little kid – maybe four years old – I've seen the day before. His mum had hung a 'HOMELESS' sign around his neck and he was making good money out of it. So I get a scrap of cardboard that's lying on the footpath and make a sign, 'NEED SHOES PLEASE'. I take my runners off and hide them in my pack. I put my cap, open side up, on the footpath. People are pretty generous.

I've got the world's coldest feet, but I've almost made $10. I'm dreaming of spending up big somewhere, when Dad walks outside. Bye-bye dreams. Dad says, *You're not going to be one of these losers.* He chucks my sign in a rubbish bin. I'm thinking, *Too late, Dad. I think we're already losers.* But I'd never say it. Not ever.

Dad walks me down to Fergus and makes me hand over my fortune. *This man gives the world something for their money*, Dad says.

Dad's right. Fergus is blind and plays the bagpipes in front of Myer. Every time we hear Fergus playing, Dad says, *Those bagpipes do the crying for you.*

Sunday May 28th, Heritage Hotel

Weekends are bad. Do too much thinking when I'm stuck inside. Had a bad dream about Crystal last night. I hate her guts. Dad's always saying it's wrong to hate. I can usually forgive, but not her. Can't ever forgive her for what she did to us.

We hadn't been back long from McKenzie's and we were skint. The last few days before Dad collects his sole parent benefit are always extra tough. If we hadn't been so low on money we wouldn't have gone to Cash Converters. Sure, we've been to plenty of these places before, but this time Dad was going to trade in his wedding ring and the gold watch that his parents gave him for his 21st. It hurt to see those things go into the cabinet with other people's bits and pieces. Still hurts. Specially the ring.

Dad told me not to get upset. That we had six months to get them back.

But we'd never got anything back before. It didn't seem worth it for just $120.

Instead of hanging out at Rosie's bus for a feed, this particular night we went to Maccas for a bit of a splurge. Dad was sitting there counting out the remainder of his fortune – a little pile of ten-dollar notes (eleven of them) and one gold coin – when this chick dressed in jeans and a stretchy top came and sat at our table. I've got to admit, she was pretty, but you could see from a mile off that she was trying to get around Dad. Could he see that? No way.

Could you lend me some money? she says with tears in her big mascara eyes. *My boyfriend ran off and took my purse.*

Why would he do that? Dad asks, really shocked.

Because they're both as bad as each other, I'm thinking. But what's the point of opening my mouth? Dad's a sucker for other people in trouble.

Then comes the story. The boyfriend's into drugs. She can't pay her rent. The landlady's chucked her out. *Name's Crystal, by the way.*

When Dad invites Crystal to stay the night in our room, I just don't feel good about it. She's all palsy with me and ruffles my hair.

She says, *Move over Leonardo DiCaprio, here comes Pete the sweet.*

I don't smile, but she doesn't get the hint that she's not wanted.

Yak, yak, yak. How she has time to breathe beats me. Yak down the street. Yak up the stairs to Room 19.

Dad rushes me off to the toilet and into my sleeping bag on the lumpy single bed. I turn over. I'm looking at the cracked wall plaster. You can see pictures in it when you stare long enough. I've tied Mum's ribbon round my wrist and I put my favourite Thomas the Tank Engine under my pillow (very uncool, but anything to do with Mum is kind of special). I pretend to sleep.

Slobber, slobber. Whisper, whisper.

Dad reads Crystal some of his poetry and then turns the lights out.

Sproing, sproing go the bed springs on the other bed.

Next morning, no Crystal. Wallet missing from Dad's trousers. No backpacks, which means Dad's poetry is gone because he always put it there. Just that one beach poem is left because it was stuck inside a book Dad had on the table.

Things I lost for ever from my backpack:

The fat controller, all my tank engines (except for Thomas) and my Thomas video which Mum and Dad gave me for my third birthday. Mum and I must have watched my Thomas video about a billion times. Mum liked Ringo Starr's pommy voice.

My photo of Mum

My school books and diary from McKenzie's

My collection of 27 Happy Meal toys

A card Mum made for my sixth birthday

My collection of straws, paper napkins, pepper and salt sachets from every take-away place we've been to.

And there was Dad sitting on his bed bawling and shouting, *Tool of the Evil One!*

Uncle Jack was the only one I could talk to about Crystal. He said, *Don't you worry, young fellah. That bad woman will get what she deserves. I have a vision of you finding your people one day. I can see you being happy.* I'm not exactly sure what he meant, but I'm hanging on to his words.

Will go for a walk before Neville etc. get back.

Monday May 29th, Heritage Hotel

Dad didn't sleep last night. He kept turning the torch on and checking out the far corners of the shed. He's been asleep most of today. I feel I've got to keep a lookout, but what for? Dad gets the messages, but I have to do the managing. It was the same with the Crystal business.

We were sitting there in Room 19. I've got my arm round Dad's shoulder. He's crying like he's never going to stop. I say, *It'll be okay, Dad.* And I decide to visit one of the charity places on our hit list.

They'll give us food vouchers and clothes. I choose the Smith family. The man who runs the place knows us from before our McKenzie's time and doesn't ask too many questions. That's how Dad likes it. Dad's still too upset to talk. I do the explaining. I tell the man about just getting back to Melbourne from New South Wales and about Crystal (skip the embarrassing bits, though) and the man tells Dad I'm bright. *Expresses himself well. He'll go a long way.* Dad smiles for the first time that day.

Every time I think of the man saying that, I get reminded of my sixth birthday when we were a proper family in our Willow Hill cottage. It's weird how long ago that feels – like sixty years, not six. And old, bald, nearly blind Miss Weiss came across from next door with the Kirschtorte she made every single year and she stayed to watch me blow out the candles on my cake. I liked the way Mum called Miss Weiss my *all-purpose grandparent* on account of Mum's mum and dad being dead and Dad's folks being somewhere way over in Western Australia. Dad says that's three thousand miles away so no wonder I've never met them. When I blow out my candles in one breath, Mum and Dad hug me and Miss Weiss takes a photo. Then Miss Weiss calls out, *Speech, Liebling, speech!* Miss Weiss always called me *mein Liebling*. So I climb on the table and give a speech that lasts so long that everyone has to sit down on chairs. And at the end when I'm bowing and everyone is clapping and cheering, Mum says to Miss Weiss and Dad, *Pete's got a way with words.*

Of all the things Crystal pinched, it's the photo of Mum I miss most of all. You can't get that back.

I've put a margarine container in Merv and Merrie's home. It has a front and back door cut out of the sides. I've put some grass and newspaper in there, too. Merv's a bit of a home-maker. He keeps tearing up the newspaper and dragging it round in circles to make a nest.

Tuesday May 30th, Heritage Hotel

Dad told me a few minutes back that he's *One of the Chosen.* I really, really need someone to speak to.

Don't think I can handle much more sneaking about inside this shed.

Wednesday May 31st, Heritage Hotel

Burning in the chest and back. Eyes strange. Have told Dad something's wrong. Dad doesn't want to take me to a doctor. He's afraid the medical authorities will turn us in.

Hope like anything it's not going to be like that time when we were living in Silver Streams caravan park. Just before I turned eight. And Dad got appendicitis. Ted from the next-door caravan drove him to hospital. Dad made a fuss about filling in the sheet. *This is an invasion of privacy.* He would only give his name and birthdate. Even though he was lying there groaning on the waiting-room seats, he wouldn't give the nurses any more information. I thought Dad might die. I kept saying, *Please, Dad.* But Dad just shook his head.

In the end, the doctor had to rush Dad into the operating theatre without the papers properly filled out. He spent one day in hospital and then he got a fright when some nurses started asking him questions, so he got himself out three days earlier than he should have. I don't know how he managed to walk out the door, but he did. I bet if I have to go to hospital, Dad will get me out early.

Just as well Dad did leave, though. Those two nights I spent with Ted were weird. Dad had told me that Ted had a good heart. I love Dad, but he gets things wrong sometimes. He got Ted badly wrong.

Every time I see a film about early convict days,

I think of Ted. He had long greasy hair, acne scars like moon craters in his face, orange teeth and long, seriously dirty fingernails. His voice was the creepiest thing, though. That low sort of growl. Like he was trying to hypnotise you.

Ted had told Dad he would look after me. But from the start I knew that was a lie when he bought a pizza and ate the lot in front of me. He gave me cheese on toast. *Yer old man was s'posed to leave me money to look after ya.* His caravan was full of smoke – tobacco and pot. He smoked a lot of pot. He'd say these really stupid things like, *Hit a 'roo today and it was still wrigglin' when I drove off* and think he was funny. I laughed 'cos I was scared not to.

Ted lost his sense of humour the next night when he ran out of pot. He started shouting, *You've got to my weed, y'little turd, haven't ya?* He banged out of the van, got in his car and didn't come back till the next morning.

I was that glad Dad got himself out of hospital quickly.

Thursday June 1st, Heritage Hotel

Pains in back getting worse. Hard to breathe. Don't want to die in this crap tin hut.

Friday June 2nd, Heritage Hotel

Dad's vit. C not enough.

Saturday June 3rd, Heritage Hotel

Dad's talking, but not to me.
Mum, I need you.

5

Monday June 12th, Daph and Bill Flynn's – Fitzroy, Melbourne

Have escaped Heritage Hotel. Had to pretty well die to do it. Pneumonia, they reckon. The pains in my back felt like little knives. But it was when I found it hard to breathe that Dad must have got worried 'cos he said, *Oh, Lord, protect my little lamb.* Then he started packing. He did what I asked, no questions, when I said I wanted my diary and Merv and Merrie to go with us.

Dad carried me on his back out of the valley in the middle of a storm. Was so sick, I couldn't have cared less. To get to the Flynns in Fitzroy, the old part of inner Melbourne, we had to catch a bus, a train and then a taxi.

Getting out of the taxi and seeing Daph and Bill's

terrace house felt good. Safe. My favourite bit is the little attic window three storeys up. It looks like this tall, narrow castle. But it was seriously late and Bill went off his head a bit while Dad was standing dripping water on the doorstep. *You always choose moments like this when we can't turn you away*, he said. Bill might be small as a jockey, but he's got a loud voice. Dad said, *Just one night*. He always says that, even if we end up staying weeks with someone. Daph's a head taller than her husband, Bill. And even though she's almost sixty, she's strong and big like a footballer. *He's as sick as a dog*, she said, and she lifted me out of Dad's arms like I weighed nothing. I reckon when I'm old, what I'll remember about Daph is her fluffy cardigans and her smell of Scent of Violets. I know that's the name, 'cos she's always got a bottle of the stuff on her bathroom cabinet. Felt like I'd come home when she was carrying me through the house. Leant my head on that soft cardigan and thought I'd die happy breathing in those violets.

Daph got the doctor straightaway. He gave me some injection and said I should go to hospital. I heard Dad arguing with everyone about danger and not letting me go to hospital. He started swearing. He never swears, usually. Dad won. The doctor left some tablets and a script. Daph's as good as any nurse anyway.

Merv and Merrie are out the back in the toolshed. Bill's put them in a cardboard fruit box with a lid. He's divided the box with a cardboard wall down the middle. Bill says none of us could cope with babies at the moment. Anyway, I think they need a break from each other. They seem a bit calmer. Every day, I spend a bit of time handling and watching them. It's funny how they clean themselves. They scratch behind their ears with their back legs. Dogs do that, too. And they wash their faces with their front paws. Just like tiny hands.

Tuesday June 13th, Daph and Bill's

Been here almost two weeks now. Legs are wobbly, but Daph's cooking is pumping the energy back into me. Look out, world.

I've always loved this place. Daph's lucky to have grown up here, and stayed on living here after she married Bill. Daph says she had her nan and her mum and dad here till they died of old age. It makes the house a real family castle.

Dad's got the attic room. I'm in Frank's new room. Small but cosy. Since the last of Daph and Bill's three daughters got married, Frank got to choose a bedroom seeing he's Daph and Bill's only son. Bill's a bit gruff, but he's fair. He said that as their boy is up the bush doing his plumbing apprenticeship, I may as well have the sunniest bedroom, which is downstairs across the passage from the kitchen. The window looks out the back. I can see a stone courtyard with a big wooden fence and a gate going into the alley behind. The yard's not that big. There's a clothes line, and there's the toolshed where Merv and Merrie are being kept in their box, and all over the place there are lots of Daph's pot plants. Right now there are white sheets flapping on the line like sails on boats.

This room's awesome. Blue walls. Polished floorboards. Plenty of shelves with books and model cars and a sound system with remote control. There's a pinboard for Frank's photos, karate and soccer certificates, and a very nice poster of Elle.

Me and Elle go back a long way. Dad says that when I was about five I pointed at her in a magazine and asked if that was Bloody Elle. She's an old friend. I don't mind sharing the room with her.

Am lying on my bed in the sun. Frank's into *The Lord of the Rings*. Started getting into it this morning. Excellent. Have just had a look at Frank's model Ferrari sports. It's red. The doors open and the headlights work. While I'm writing, I've got Led Zeppelin on the sound system.

Everything is clean and tidy. Feel good with things tidy.

List of things to do later today:
Check on Merv and Merrie. Clean out their poo.
Give them fresh food and water.
Sit outside for a while and do some drawing.
Help Daph make a cake.
Watch TV.

Wednesday June 14th, Daph and Bill's

Went to the Vic market today with Daph. Had a bit of trouble getting Dad to let me go. In the end he said yes as long as I wore a green coat and yellow tracky pants. He says everyone is wearing either green or yellow and that I'm to blend in. Daph just looked fed up, but it worries me.

The market is a lot of fun. All these stalls under this massive tin roof with open sides. Must take up a whole city block. You can get anything there. Clothes. Watches. Cameras. Cheap as. But the vegetable part is best. Loud and stinky and squashy. It's like an auction – all the stall owners yelling at you to buy their stuff, *Bargain, lady!* Daph barters. She likes to get the best price. I'm staggering along behind carrying her bags, treading on the vegies that have been dropped. And we're pushing through crowds of people from heaps and heaps of different countries of the world.

The really good thing about getting out was the

way Daph started talking about Mum. Never knew Daph and Bill went so far back. How before Mum married, she was doing some music course and she and two other students rented next door to Daph's. Daph said you could hear Mum practising her singing any time of the day or night. Daph was like a mother to her. Mum used to go with Daph to the Vic market once a week. Just the two of them. Was glad to hear her talking about Mum.

And it was really good hearing about how Mum and Dad met at the Fitzroy Arms where locals and students hang out. Daph and Bill still go there for a drink. And about Mum playing guitar and singing and Dad reciting poetry there. And Dad getting down on his knees in front of the whole pub to ask Mum to marry him and everyone going wild and cheering. Daph said, *Your mum was the best thing that ever happened to Michael. She kept him sensible.*

Have been wondering what Daph means when she said Mum kept Dad *sensible.* How come I can't keep him sensible?

Thursday June 15th, Daph and Bill's

Lorraine and Simone visited today. Daph, Lorraine, Simone – grandma, daughter, granddaughter – three generations of giant females.

Lorraine looks extra gi-normous with those twins inside her. Spoils the fun knowing already that they're a girl and boy. Daph's excited, though. That'll make three grandkids. I bet Simone will get jealous. Nine years is a big gap. Considering she uses me as a punching bag, I can't see Simone doing much baby rocking.

Simone is seriously rough. And she's definitely going to be as big as Daph. Dad has always said I can't hit back and that Simone will grow out of it. But I've known her since she was crawling and even then she pulled my hair so hard a tuft came out. Anyway, I can mostly handle Simone now. She likes my stories, specially when I make her the hero all the time.

Soon as I saw Simone today, she runs up and says, *Punch or a story!* But Dad made me go into his room until she and Lorraine left. Felt a fool sitting in there listening to Simone thumping round the house and asking everyone, *Why can't Pete come and play? We haven't seen him for a whole year.* When I asked why I couldn't even talk to Simone, Dad said, *It's best not too many people know where we are.* It doesn't add up, but I can't upset Dad by saying this.

What sort of danger is this when you can't even trust old friends?

Friday June 16th, Daph and Bill's

Dad's been watching the news each night like his life depends on it. Last night he told me he's getting messages from world leaders like the Pope and the Queen. They are warning Dad about the spies from Asio who are after him. The spies are hunting him down from unmarked government cars and helicopters. They're also tapping into any phone calls he makes. I'm not to tell Daph and Bill. They wouldn't understand.

How come I don't understand, either? I look at the same programmes as Dad, and I can't see or hear any messages. But then Dad says the world leaders speak in code. Dad isn't dumb. He'd know, wouldn't he? Wish I could tell Daph, but I don't want her thinking badly of Dad. Daph and Bill have been good to both of us.

Quiet day. Really getting into *The Lord of the Rings*.

Saturday June 17th, Daph and Bill's

Every time I show my face in the kitchen, Daph feeds me. Good playing cricket with Bill. But playing out the back alley isn't as good as at McKenzie's with Vic. If you play on the hard, wet sand at low tide you can get a fantastic spin. And if you're fielding on soft sand, you can throw yourself at the ball and do these brilliant catches without worrying about how you fall. Last game we had, I caught Vic out and landed flat on my back at the same time.

Daph and Bill are nice, but they've been arguing a lot with Dad. As long as I stay quiet and don't move, people carry on talking in front of me. It works extra well if they think I'm watching TV or reading. They forget I'm there.

One of the main arguments is because Dad keeps telling Daph and Bill that he's getting guidance from the Bible. Daph reckons that opening the Bible at any place and sticking your finger on the page is not guidance but *pure folly*. She says it's not a lucky dip, but it's like a driver's manual that needs to be read carefully. Daph's the religious one. Bill reckons any kind of religion is dangerous. Daph asked if learning how to love was dangerous. Not sure what Daph meant by that, but Bill walked out of the room saying that every time Dad was here it caused trouble. Thinking about that, he does end up falling out with most of the people we have stayed with.

Glad I've got Frodo's adventures to get into. It's like Gollum's ring. It helps me vanish.

Sunday June 18th, Daph and Bill's

Today's argument is about me and school. Daph keeps telling Dad to settle down and let me go back to school. That I need the friendship. Have been listening carefully to these discussions because I wouldn't mind school again even if it does mean school number five. Am fed up with being lonely. But Dad's stubborn. He says he's *considering lots of options*. Daph just sighs.

Half an hour ago, asked Dad what these 'options' are. Said he'd tell me when he's received the correct guidance. It's round in circles stuff with Dad.

Back to Frodo for me. This ring we thought was so amazing in *The Hobbit* might be a bit evil. It changes the person who wears it too long and you don't know it's happening to you. That's a scary thought. Something happening to you and you don't know.

Monday June 19th, Daph and Bill's

Just now heard Bill in the kitchen saying to Dad, *We've known you almost fifteen years and you've got less common sense now than you did back then.*

And Dad said, *Back off, Bill, there's things I could tell you but I'm not able yet. Just believe me. The boy is being looked after the best I know how. We are in danger and only I know the extent of it.*

Tuesday June 20th, Heritage Hotel

Worst day for a long time. Even worse than getting to Daph and Bill's a couple of weeks back.

Can't be sure how it started. I was out the back. When I walk in the kitchen, Dad is chucking a wobbly with Daph. *She was not a bird in a gilded cage!!!* He spits the words. Really spits. Bits of spit are pinging out of his mouth.

Bill has just got back with his morning paper from the corner shop. He's standing in the doorway and shouting at Dad, *For crying out loud, we're the only ones who'll put up with your crap. Will you stop stabbing us in the back!*

That's all he says. Dad looks at Bill as if he's the Devil himself.

You said the key word! screams Dad.

What damned key word? asks Bill. *All I said was to stop stabbing us in the back. You know – betraying our friendship.*

You said it again, screams Dad, grabbing me by the arm. *You said STAB.*

What's the matter with STAB? asks Bill, again.

Dad doesn't wait around. He takes me to my room and makes me pack. Have to really beg to get Merv and Merrie, but he lets me in the end. I don't think they like going back into their ice-cream container. This time, Merrie bites me on the finger. Dad goes upstairs, gets his gear from his room and shoves it any old how in his pack. Next thing we walk out the door and Dad slams it so hard I can feel the hundred-year-old bricks vibrate. He's standing in the street and yelling at the shut door, *The Lord will smite thee!*

I have to lead Dad away.

After Daph's place, this kerosene-tin shed seems more of a hole than ever.

What the heck does *gilded* mean?

6

Wednesday June 21st, Heritage Hotel

Dad's gone quiet. I have lots to think about, myself. Questions I want to ask:

Why won't Dad get a real job and look after me properly?

Why so many fights with people everywhere we go?

Why can't he trust me enough to tell me the whole story?

I'm feeling dead-set angry. I've never felt this way about Dad.

I'm angry and sad as all hell at the same time.

Thursday June 22nd, Train to the city

Goodbye Heritage Hotel.

Neville's dad sprung us. About sunset, Dad let

me out for a leak. Was watering my favourite tree when this man came walking up from the sheep paddock. I made a run for the door, but he was faster. He grabbed me hard by both arms. Was bellowing for Dad who came running out of the shed. Meanwhile, Neville's dad is yelling, *You've got some explaining to do or I'll be getting the police! Firstly, what's your name? And give me proof of your identity.*

Dad fumbles around in his wallet. He gets out his sole parent benefit card and holds it up. *Sinclair, is it? Well we're the Collinses and you are trespassing on Collins property.*

By now we have an audience. The rest of the Collins family have come out of their house into the backyard. They stand behind Mr Collins as if we are too dangerous to get close to. This is better than a TV soapie for Neville. He's enjoying himself. But I bet he wouldn't like to know how much I could tell about him and his whimpy whingeing ways.

Please understand. We've been travelling and we got low on money, Dad pleads.

On the run from trouble, I'll bet, says Mr Collins.

It's not like you think, says Dad. *I'm a law abiding man. Man's law and God's law.*

Oh, sure, says Mr Collins.

Believe me, says Dad.

I believe him, Max, says Mrs Collins.

You're a sandwich short of a picnic, mate. Get your stuff and get out, orders Mr Collins as he shoves me towards Dad. *You've got twenty minutes.*

Don't give away information to the enemy, Dad whispers as we scramble around inside the shed stuffing our gear into packs. I make sure Mervin and Merrie are safely stowed away in their container at the top of my pack. I can hear Mrs Collins trying to convince her husband to order a taxi for us to help us to the train station. She wins.

The family escort us to the street. The taxi arrives quickly. Mrs Collins gives the driver some money and puts a twenty-dollar note into Dad's hand. *Train fares*, she says. *Good luck.*

As I step into the taxi, Neville hisses, *You're a couple of spongers.*

The taxi drives a few metres down the road. I'll never forget looking behind. The Collins are still gawking. I stick my arm out the window and give them the rude finger.

Our train is going click-clackety into the night. Pinpricks of rain are hitting the windows. Have just asked Dad where we'll be sleeping tonight. He isn't answering. He's not there. He's an empty room. At least, I thought he couldn't hear me. Just then he said, *The voices say to keep to the river.*

More friggin' voices. Why can't the voices tell us to go to the Hilton?

This is the pits. A winter night on the Yarra.

I HATE MY LIFE.

Friday June 23rd, John and Karen's

Last night was hell. The worst. The very worst. I'm missing you so badly, Dad. Where have they taken you?

At the police station, when the Human Services people came to take me away, they said you were going to hospital. Is this what you have been trying to protect me from? You were calling out my name. I'm sorry, Dad. You were right about needing to hide.

But huddling under that bridge, trying to keep out of the winter rain, wasn't a great idea. Pretty disgusting having to share it with that alcoholic who had shat his pants and those two super-agitated druggies – that tall curly-haired blond guy and the really pretty girl. Don't think she'd be much older than I am. It's really 'cos of them that this has all happened.

Hate seeing druggies doing their thing with a spoon held over a candle flame and then all the rest. The alco was all right. He kept telling them off. Things

76

like, *Yous'll kill yourselves, y'know*. But anything he said just got them more uptight. They were abusing him something awful.

Shut your f'n mouth hole you useless bag of stink.

But he wouldn't shut up. *You're still young. Yous'll be breaking some mum's heart.*

That got to the girl. She walked up to the alco who was lying on his side and started kicking him in the stomach and telling him he'd asked for it. The smell of the rain on stone, candle smoke, shit and vomit. Foul. And Dad yelling this almighty big *NO!* which stopped the girl for only a second. Then she got this vicious, ugly look on her face and I knew Dad was in for it. Just knew it.

Next thing the police are there with their torches. Blinding our eyes. It's Dad and me they seem to be coming for. Everything Dad has warned me about is true. But my mind is made up. They're not going to get us.

I grab Dad's arm and get him moving. We're running along the footpath beside the river. Running so hard it's burning in the lungs. Running with my pack on. Back is still sore today from that pack thumping into me. You can hear feet behind us. Cop feet pounding along. But I'm young and Dad has long, thin runner's legs. He used to be a champion athlete at school. We can do it. There's the city gardens up ahead to our right. If we can get amongst the trees we'll be safe.

The two of us give it all we've got. Without wasting a moment to look back, I know we're beating the cop because I hear those big feet slowing down. Just then a helicopter comes chopping its way over the tall city buildings. Dad looks up, swerves and hits a mossy bit on the concrete. My dad is falling into the water. Sideways into the dark water. He's going to drown. He's truly going to drown. He can run, but he never learnt to swim.

Dad's head surfaces and his arms are splashing about. I chuck the backpack and throw myself into the river. Straight at Dad.

Dad grabs hold, but it's like he's trying to stand on me. I'm being pulled under. And it's so cold, so ice cold. We're going to drown. Both of us. But I'm remembering when Vic and I used to pretend to rescue each other for fun in the lagoon. And it comes to me what I have to do.

Dad's hands are iron tight, but somehow I get up to gulp some air and then I go down under. With one leg I kick at Dad as hard as I can. I think I get him in the groin. His hands let go and I swim free. At the moment he's about to go down again, I get behind and grab him by his ponytail. *On your back!* I shout. Dad tries. This time I keep free of him, but I don't let go of his hair. I'm dragging him to the stone wall of the river.

The helicopter is right over the top of us. Its searchlight is beaming straight on us. Like the spotlight in a stage show. Big cop hands reach down and haul Dad up. I find footholds in the wall and pull myself out. Then they take us to the police station.

I don't know where the hospital is that you're in.

I've got to find someone who'll listen to me. People need to understand. You're loving to me. Kind to strangers. Clever with words and with making things. What's the big deal about being a bit different?

Everyone here is being nice to me but it makes no difference. I've still got my pack and this diary. They've let me keep Merv and Merrie's house next to my bed. They've also got me some brand new clothes. Socks, jocks, pyjamas, two tracksuits, runners. Everything.

I'll always hate these clothes. They feel like funeral clothes.

The things I was made to wear after I was taken from my dad.

Where are you, Dad?

Saturday June 24th, John and Karen's

Human Services have sent me to stay with a family. They're trying to be friendly. Even their kids. But I heard the little bloke who I share a room with ask his dad how come I just write in my book all the time and never want to go out and play.

Still eat what they put in front of me. Thought if you felt like your life had ended, you would stop doing everything.

What are you doing today, Dad?

I know you're thinking about me.

Sunday June 25th, John and Karen's

Karen says you're sick and that you can't look after me while you're in hospital. She asked if I understood your sickness. I nodded to get rid of her, to stop her saying those things. But I don't really understand.

Karen told me I'll be going to the children's court tomorrow and I'll get to meet my solicitor. I can tell him what I want to happen. Then on Tuesday there's this other court thing. I'll have a solicitor and you'll have a solicitor. The magistrate will decide what's happening to me. Why?

The man and the lady who took me away will be there, too. The ones from Human Services. Doesn't sound very human to me. Why can't they leave us alone? We were all right.

Have been thinking about the day after we first met, Vic. I'm skipping stones across a big rock pool and you walk up and say, *Wanna see something?* And I say, *Sure.* And we walk round the rocks to this cliff going thirty metres straight up. When you start climbing, I want to say, *No way.* But I just follow. When we're halfway up, you say, *Don't never ever look down.* So of course I look down. Down, down below is the rock platform and the waves crashing on to it. I picture falling thirty metres and splatting. I'm nearly pooing myself. Just have to keep going up.

Half an hour later, we're close to where that pair of sea eagles have their big twig nest. It's on a bit of a shelf just below the top of the cliff. One of the eagles swoops right near us, and the length of its wings is the height of a man (that's if the man was lying sideways). We scramble on to this narrow ledge and sit for ages watching. Those eagles are something, gliding up there on the wind currents and then diving down to the sea to catch fish with their talons. But for me it's getting back down the cliff that's the tough bit. Climbing down blind. Just feeling with your hands and feet. That's what it's like. And I freeze. My skeleton would still be clinging there right now if you hadn't stuck by me. *No worries. I was like this the first time*, you say. Hand, foot, hand, foot. You spend an hour talking me down like something out of *Police Rescue*.

That's how I am now. Hanging off a cliff. Trying to get down. Doing it blind. And I'm telling myself, *Hand, foot, hand, foot. Don't look down. Just keep going and it'll be all right.*

Monday June 26th, John and Karen's

Little Lonsdale St is one part of Melbourne I never want to see again. Dead certain. The children's court building is a big glass fish tank for weirdo humans. From outside I could see this man dressed in torn jeans and work boots throwing a spas in the foyer. He was thumping the walls. Two men in uniforms were trying to talk to him. When Karen and I walked through the sliding doors, you could hear him yelling about his rights as a father.

Upstairs where you hang around before getting called to court was just as bad. Everyone was sad. All these grown-ups crying or arguing or yelling at their kids or just sitting there looking blank. And talk about a wait.

To fill in the time, I played 'spot the official'. It's easy to play. The social workers, solicitors and court officials – men and ladies – were dressed in dark suits. Then there were the security men and policemen who were in uniform. That left the others like me who had to be there. Some dressed nice and did their hair neat, but it looked try-hard. And some couldn't give a stuff. Stained clothes. Any old things on their feet. I saw one lady in slippers.

After about an hour, the Human Services lady turned up – the one who made me stay at John and Karen's. Her name's Teresa. She was all smiley with me, but she couldn't get me to smile back. I won't be a traitor to Dad. Teresa took me and Karen into a room to talk privately. She said the solicitor would listen to what I want and tell the magistrate tomorrow. She asked me if I understood about Dad. I'm getting jacked off about being reminded. Did I know that he has a mental illness? I just nodded. My dad insane? He's not a bad person. Why take me away from him? If they take me away, I'll have no one.

Karen and I must have sat there another hour before I saw the solicitor. His name is Greg. He's young. Tall, blue eyes, smart dresser.

Told Greg my dad wasn't a bad man. Why did he have to go to court like a criminal? Greg said Dad wasn't being punished, but he needed to be made to get well. He doesn't know he's sick. Greg said he was there to explain to the judge what I want.

Things I told Greg:

Dad to get better soon.

Me to see Dad whenever I want.

Not to have to live with Karen and John.

To talk to Daph and Bill on the phone.

BUT WHAT I REALLY, REALLY WANT AND GREG DIDN'T WRITE THIS DOWN IS FOR ALL THESE PEOPLE TO LEAVE US ALONE. DAD NEEDS ME. I NEED DAD. STOP MESSING WITH US.

Tuesday June 27th, John and Karen's

Mum's dead. Dad's good as dead.

Day began with a shock. Was sitting there in the waiting area at the children's court. Dad walked in the door. His clothes looked more raggedy than usual. He was dark under the eyes. There was this man sticking by him like a prison guard. But I'll always remember that my dad walked tall like a king. He moved through the crowd of squabbling grown-ups, screaming kids and busy court workers as if they weren't there.

Dad noticed me, though. Came straight towards me and hugged me. He had tears in his eyes.

Are you okay, my boy? he asked. *I'll get you out*

of this. Don't worry. I have direct communication with powerful people.

Who's telling the truth? Dad's the most caring father you could have. He loves me and I love him.

That's not good enough for the court, though. We had to go into this big room with a high-up throne. The magistrate sits up there. Everyone called her *Your Worship*. And they bowed to her like she was God or something. I thought there might be a jury, but there was only Dad, me, our two solicitors, Dad's guard (who turned out to be a nurse), Karen, the two Human Services people, a man who typed everything we said on to a computer, another man who announced everything, and this Worship person.

What made me angry today was the way the Human Services man put together a story about Dad and me that was only half the truth. About Mum deserting us and then dying soon after in a car crash. About Dad having had no fixed address for nearly six years and me going to four different schools and it being three years since I last went to school. About Dad's life not being good for my safety or health and me needing a 'stable environment'. About Dad needing his health 'managed' before he can look after me. Dad's kept us safe from those people who took Mum. He should be father of the year, not locked away.

Everyone seems to think that if you don't live exactly the same way as everyone else, then something's wrong. Wish the De Lucias were here to explain that you can do it differently.

Was sitting there next to Dad, thinking all that about the De Lucias and Dad and me, when the magistrate started saying what she'd decided. Dad looked scared stiff. I squeezed his hand.

That lady sure has power. She was using it to keep Dad away from me. Am allowed to visit him once a week in hospital and ring him every day. But they are calling me 'long term'. Sounds like a jail sentence for murder. It means I'll be moving from Karen's to someplace else.

My hands were shaking so much I had to sit on them. Was trying to look cool, like I couldn't care less what they did to me. Wouldn't let them see I'm shattered. Next everyone was standing and bowing to the Worship person. The nurse led Dad off. He kept looking back at me.

Greg says he'll try to find Daph and Bill's phone number for me. I'm allowed to ring Greg whenever I like.

Karen lost it with me tonight for making marks on her table with my dinner knife. I didn't even know I was doing that. She also told me I'm leaving. I won't have to live with her and John any more. I'm going to be fostered by people called Mr and Mrs Cowper. What's the difference between fostered and adopted? They're just pulling me further from Dad.

Big question of the year. Why hasn't Dad ever properly explained to me about Mum? Who abducted and killed her? Or did she walk out on us like the Human Services man said? Did Dad do something I don't know about? I can't swallow that. And if Mum was really leaving she'd have written a note. It would be plain cruel to leave your family without a note. Mum wasn't cruel. Anyway, Dad now says he doesn't even believe she did die. That's why I'm not allowed to talk about it with him or even remind him that we did go to the funeral.

Still wondering what gilded means.

7

EMAIL
From: Prue Cowper
To: Allison and Neil Cowper
Sent: Wed 28/06/00
Subject: News!

Dear Allison and Neil,

Taupo sounds blissful. N.Z. weather is being kind to you. Melbourne's pretty miserable at the moment. It's a sensible plan to stay a bit longer with Ida and Ted. You'll need to be in top form when you get back, because you are now officially foster grandparents!

His name is Peter Sinclair. He's tall for his age (12) — gypsy looks — tousled dark brown hair, grey-blue eyes. He's as cagey as hell, but we're rapt! Human Services tell us he's super-bright —

really gifted and really high IQ! He's a reader and a writer apparently. We really want to see him on his feet.

Our social life will have to come to a stop for the moment, but it's worth it. Godfrey's being fantastic.

Much love,

Prue

Wednesday June 28th, Prue and Godfrey's

Karen didn't look too sad to see me go this morning. Maybe Karen's place wasn't as bad as I thought. Teresa drove me and my pack with Merv, Merrie and other stuff over here this afternoon. As usual, she tried to get me to talk, but I made sure my face looked fuzzy, like a TV that's stuffed. She asked me for the five billionth time, *Are you sure you understand about your dad's mental illness?* I nodded my head. *Here we go again*, I thought.

This is my long-term placement. Prue and Godfrey Cowper are rich. Prue is thin, blonde and quite good-looking considering she must be in her thirties. She wears lots of gold chains and bracelets. I heard her telling Teresa how she and Godfrey work out at the gym every week. Godfrey's got really short brown hair and he's built. It's hard to imagine either of them sweating. They look expensive.

We're somewhere close to the city, but there's lots of trees in the streets. When Teresa was driving me here, I saw people jogging, bike riding or walking their dogs. The whole lot of them looked like some TV ad for the perfect life.

Same with Prue and Godfrey. They have a brand new house – a white, two-storey box with this massive front door and a tree in a pot on each side of it. The trees have these useless-looking small oranges on them. Teresa was raving on about their *lovely home* and Prue tells her there are five bedrooms and three bathrooms and a whole lot of other rooms.

Godfrey and Prue took us on a guided tour. Showed off the in-ground swimming pool and the BBQ area out the back. Took us up to my bedroom. Have my own desk, computer and a sound system better than Frank's. I'm thinking, what sort of job do you need to have a place like this? Teresa must be thinking the same 'cos she asks Godfrey and Prue what they *do for a crust*. Prue is a consultant – whatever that means – and Godfrey is an accountant.

After Teresa left, Prue and Godfrey gave me steamed fish with salad followed by fruit and soy yoghurt. Ate the fish, left the salad. Ate the fruit salad after scraping off the yoghurt. Have this horrible feeling they're into health food.

Survived the meal, but then came the get-to-know-you session in the family room. Now that's a strange name to call that room, because it turns out Prue and Godfrey haven't got kids. They can't have kids. I'm their first foster child.

We think it's cool we've got a kid coming to stay, says Prue.

And a fine one too, says Godfrey.

What a pair of try-hards.

What if they want me to call them Mum and Dad or something? No way.

Rang Dad at the hospital tonight. He was freaked out. Kept telling me I had to get him out of there. That the doctors had made a mistake and this is all part of Asio's conspiracy against him.

There just might be something the matter with Dad. None of the other grown-ups I meet are frightened. How do you get rid of fear?

Friday June 30th, Prue and Godfrey's

Nothing much to say about the last two days. Has rained a lot. Prue took yesterday and today off work to help me settle in. Stayed in my room as much as possible. Read a couple of books Prue gave me. Way too happy-ever-after. Did some drawing, thought, listened to music, played on the computer, fed Merv and Merrie who are still in their ice-cream-container home. Watched them nibbling each other's fur. Then Merrie started chasing Mervin around and making his life hell. Only came down for meals. Prue and Godfrey didn't hassle me too much. This room is a dream come true, but my life sucks. Everything sucks.

Found a dictionary tonight. Gilded means 'thinly covered with gold'.

Mum was in a golden cage. And so am I.

Saturday July 1st, Prue and Godfrey's

More rain. Prue woke me early 'cos she and Godfrey wanted me to go with them to some indoor swim centre. Said no thanks. Prue's standing in the doorway smiling and jingling with jewellery when she suddenly wrinkles her little nose and says, *What's that smell?*

And I say, *What smell?*

And she says, *There's definitely a strange smell in here.*

I'm pretty sure what the definitely strange smell is, but I say, *It's probably me. You're not used to children.*

By now Prue is checking out my room like a sniffer dog. Before you know it, she's over at the desk. *What's in here?* she asks, and she yanks the lid off

Merv and Merrie's home.

Well, you should have heard the scream. All at the same time, Merv and Merrie are flying through the air and Prue's jumped on to the end of my bed. Naturally, Merv and Merrie's safety comes first, so I'm out of bed and crawling about on the floor trying to rescue them, saying, *They're only mice. They won't hurt*, and Prue's still on the bed screaming and Godfrey's appeared in the doorway yelling, *What's going on here?*

It's all sorted out now. I got Merv and Merrie back in their house. Godfrey made Prue a nice hot cup of tea. Then we had what Godfrey called a *round table discussion* about my mice. They can stay where they are for the moment, but Godfrey will make a better home for them on the back verandah.

Seeing as Prue and Godfrey were fair about Merv and Merrie, I changed my mind about the swim. Wasn't worth it, but. All these serious fitness geeks swimming up and down, up and down. Nothing like McKenzie's.

Sunday July 2nd, Prue and Godfrey's

No one believes in sleeping-in round here. Got woken up early for a walk.

Walk went okay. We went all round the neighbourhood looking at everyone else's houses and gardens. Posh. Then Prue says, *Let's have brunch.* So we end up at this trendy cafe where you eat at little tables out on the footpath. I'm sitting there with my lemon pancake and my fruit smoothie and I'm wondering what Dad's getting to eat at the hospital. I look around at the other people all dressed up and eating *brunch*. Maybe I'm not grateful enough or something, but I feel pissed off that they can live like this and not know a damn thing or give a damn about people who can't eat *brunch* and don't even know what the damn word means.

Monday July 3rd, Prue and Godfrey's

Had to get up even earlier. Prue took another day off work. Godfrey's taking off the other bit of the week. Got enrolled at Berringarra school today.

Berringarra school sucks. I'll be starting next week.

Big wire fence round the school. More buildings than space to play.

Principal, Mr Duncan, all palsy. Said he'd heard I was a good reader. Who told him, I'd like to know? Asked me if I like footie. I said, maybe. That ended the conversation.

Grade six teacher, Mrs Judith Bickerton, looks like Smaug. She tried smiling, but it seemed fake. It was like that smile might burn you.

The class was out at music, but I got to see where my desk will be. Right under the dragon's nose. Mrs Bickerton pulled out a plastic crate, slapped on a sticky label with my name written on it, and said that's where my books will get stored. She smiled her scary smile and said in a hurrying sort of way that she was looking forward to having me in the class. Sure.

Have changed my mind about wanting to be back at school. What if I'm really stupid at my work? Will this Bickerton woman make a fool of me in front of the class? What do I tell the kids about me and Dad and everything?

Don't just feel alone, the really scary thing is I *am* alone. If you stuck me on Mars and I was standing there in the dark on a rock looking down at earth, I wouldn't feel one bit more lonely than I am now.

Prue just stuck her head round the door and said she'll be taking me to see Dad tomorrow. Finally.

Tuesday July 4th, Prue and Godfrey's

Worst thing today was seeing Dad. Never thought I'd think that.

Prue drove me over to the Royal Melbourne. Had to walk through a whole lot of security doors. Ended up in a main lounge area. It's got mad people just walking around, except it's hard to tell who's a visitor and who's officially mad.

There was this lady, maybe about twenty years old, who came up to Prue and said, *They reckon it's going to be a full moon tonight. I wonder if we'll all be howling at it?* I thought that was pretty funny. Prue and I laughed and the mad lady laughed with us.

Dad wasn't laughing, though. The nurse showed me his room, but stayed outside with Prue. Dad's room sucks. A bed. A chair. A cupboard. Dad was still in the same clothes as yesterday. When I asked why, he whispered, *They're trying to get me into the shower so they can gas me.* Positive that's not true.

Dad didn't have anything else to say. We sat on his bed and he hugged me. Tried thinking of things to say. Was just talking about anything, telling him about all the stuff in my new room. Just anything. When Prue came in to tell me we had to go, I was ready to leave.

Godfrey came in from work tonight carrying a small cupboard with a front opening door. The sort of thing you might have next to a bed. *Guess what this is*, Godfrey asked me. *An old cupboard*, I said.

Well, yes and no, said Godfrey. *Found it on a road-side rubbish collection. If we knock out one of the sides and nail wire there, we'll have a Mousery.* So we found a bit of mesh wire in the garage and finished the Mousery about half an hour ago. The door will make it easy to clean out the poo.

Mice are enjoying their latest move. Mervin's eating more than usual.

Wednesday July 5th, Prue and Godfrey's

If only someone could tell me how long I have to wait for Dad to be fixed. Like is this a for ever thing and is everyone too scared to tell me the truth? It got me crying in bed last night. Eyes looked all puffy this morning. Prue wanted to know why. Told her they get all sore when I read a lot. Godfrey said seeing as Prue and I were going shopping this morning, maybe I'd like to borrow some dark glasses off him to protect me from the sunlight. Said yes. For a minute I thought Godfrey might know the truth. Really, really don't want strangers knowing. But I don't think he does, because he says his eyes sometimes get like that too.

The shopping was supposed to be for some more new clothes for me, but it also ended up being cake and coffee with one of Prue's friends, then trailing with both of them into a lingerie shop. Embarrassing. Was glad I had Godfrey's dark glasses on.

After Godfrey got back from work the three of us drove down to this place on the Yarra. We hired bikes and went for a ride until it was almost dark. Then we visited Godfrey's mum and dad for tea.

Godfrey's folks are called Allison and Neil. Allison has these two grey plaits twisted over her head. Neil has white hair and a white moustache. Godfrey's their only child. They live in a little wooden house in Box Grove and they've been there 53 years since the day they got married. There's this photo of their wedding day on the mantelpiece. They haven't changed much except Allison had two brown plaits twisted over her head and Neil had black hair and a black moustache.

They're okay. They're way more normal than Godfrey and Prue.

Allison cooked shepherd's pie and then we had apple fritters and ice cream. She kept saying, *Have some more, lovey. You're a growing boy!* So I did exactly what she said, and finished off their ice cream for them. Who knows when I'll ever get to taste the stuff again? Neil showed me his workshop up the backyard. We made a model glider plane out of wood. For a while I liked it. Then I remembered Dad. When we were leaving, Neil said, *Don't you be downhearted now*. Easy for them to say.

Dad rang after we got back tonight. Told me fruit and vegies are safe to eat. Told him about the bike ride. He said when he gets out he'll buy me my own bike. Felt like saying, *In your dreams, Dad*. But didn't.

Thursday July 6th, Prue and Godfrey's

Went to bed early last night so I could think. Ended up crying again. Glad I've got those dark glasses. Wore them all morning.

Godfrey's turn to play parent today. I'll give him 6/10. Overdoing the mates bit. Missed a couple of great moments to discipline me when I gave him a bit of cheek.

Went for run around six blocks with Godfrey. Exhausting.

Helped Godfrey put up a pinboard in my room.

Cleaned out the Mousery. I picked out Merv and Merrie by their tails – if you hold them by the base of the tail near the body and then slip your other hand underneath, it doesn't hurt them. Put in dry grass clippings, fresh food and water.

Godfrey and Prue are way too healthy with their eating. Might starve to death here if I can't get my teeth around a bit of junk food soon.

What are you doing right now, Dad? Yeah, I know. You're missing me. You need me. Now it's up to me to fix things up, except I don't know what I have to do. I'm thinking, thinking all the time. Even when I look like I'm doing something else, I'm still thinking. Need some good advice, but who can I trust?

Friday July 7th, Prue and Godfrey's

Godfrey's learning. I jacked up about helping with the dishes at lunchtime and Godfrey got heavy with me. He said, *Stop behaving like a charity case and start pulling your own weight around here.* He even threatened to send me to my room. Saved Godfrey from the hard work of carrying out his threat by picking up the tea towel. Godfrey's idea of a punishment is a bit over the top. 7/10 for effort, though.

Rang Dad. He reckons they've put poison in his food. It's only safe to have bread and water. Told him if he starves to death he won't get to see me again. I also said that if the other patients aren't dropping dead round him, then he's probably not getting poisoned. It's tough being your dad's dad.

Phone message tonight from Greg, my solicitor. He's tracked down Daph and Bill's phone number for me.

Saturday July 8th, Prue and Godfrey's

Went for fast a.m. walk with Godfrey and Prue round block. Freezing cold, but warmed up. Can think of easier ways to get warm. Fruit salad and yoghurt for breakfast.

Rang Daph and Bill. They knew about Dad. Greg had rung and told them. Asked Daph if I could come and live with them. Daph said she would have liked that, but Lorraine has had her twins early and the whole family is coming to live with Daph and Bill until Lorraine feels she can cope on her own. I said I would sleep on the sofa. Daph said I deserved my own room. Hung up. Didn't want to start crying.

Rang Dad tonight. Told him about Lorraine's twins. That got Dad remembering about when I was a baby and he did a night shift with the bottle to let Mum sleep. And then I remembered how I slept between Mum and Dad in their big bed until I was four years old. All squished. And Mum used to say I was *the jam in the sandwich*. That got Dad badly upset. *We're all we've got*, he kept saying. And that's true. We're on our own. Can't get it out of my mind.

1068236759

8

Sunday July 9th, Prue and Godfrey's

I did it because I love him and he loves me and we've only got each other and Daph and Bill don't want me and Godfrey and Prue just want to play Mummy and Daddy and they'd do that with any old kid they got. Other people might try to care, but your mum or dad loves you no matter what. He wanted to get out and it seemed right.

Don't know what he means by this Judas word. Just know it's something bad. The way he said it sounded more ugly than the F word. It sounded like dirt, dirt, dirt.

Anyway, I had to help Dad escape. We'd be better off together. And he didn't seem that sick anyway. I could handle him. And it would mean I didn't have to go to Berringarra school tomorrow.

It seemed like it was meant to be, the way Prue dropped me off at the hospital for time by myself with Dad. As soon as I got into his room I told him to get his coat.

Get your coat, Dad, I say. *We're going for a walk.*

Where to?

Outside. Right outside.

Yes, let's, says Dad. *Good boy, you understand.*

And I do. I really do understand.

We have to walk down two hallways, pass by the nurses' station near the lounge and get through two security doors to get to the outside world. I don't have a plan, but I have it fixed in my mind that my dad is going to be free. They haven't done him any good in this place anyway. We make it down the first hallway. But we turn the corner down the second and this doctor in a white coat is coming towards us. Dad mustn't panic. He must walk slow and casual.

Walk slow and casual, I tell Dad, *and don't look at him.*

Dad is hanging on to my arm. The walk slow is easy for poor Dad. His medication makes him shuffle like an old man.

The doctor is stopping to talk. He's tall and bends over us to speak. *So Michael, this must be your boy?*

Yes, this is Peter. He's taking me for a walk. Just a short walk. We're not going outside. Just inside.

Easy, Dad, I'm thinking.

Are you sure you can manage, Peter? It's like the doctor knows Dad wants to make a run for it.

I try to look the doctor in the eye, but I'm about to lie my head off so my eyes slide down to the doctor's stripy tie.

We're okay, I say to the tie.

We can easily get a nurse to walk with you, Peter. More smiling down on us.

Suddenly I realise how trapped Dad must feel.

I need to be alone with Dad. I want to tell him stuff.

The doctor smiles and nods and passes on.

Dad squeezes my arm and we keep walking.

We're in the lounge which is chockers full of patients and visitors due to it being a Sunday. Dad is tired so I get him to sit in an armchair. I have some watching to do.

I watch visitors leaving through the sliding security doors. But first they have to tell the nurse who looks at everyone in the lounge through the big glass window of the nurses' station. The nurse is like a prison guard. When a visitor is ready to go, the nurse presses some button and the doors slide open. There's no way the staff are not going to notice me and Dad. I have to break this news to Dad.

Dad, it's not going to work. I get ready to explain, but I don't finish.

The lady who just the other day was cracking

jokes about the full moon is seriously upset. She's chucking a wobbly and screaming at her visitors. At the same time a family is standing at the sliding doors waiting to leave. The nurse activates the doors and he and two others rush out of the station and head for the full-moon lady. I grab Dad's arm and we join the family as they walk to freedom. Easy as that. The second lot of doors slide open and through we go. Just the outside doors to the car park now, and then I hear it. A police siren. And through the window we see a chopper flying almost at roof level across the city. 'Cos of winter, it has got dark quickly. The chopper has a searchlight sweeping across the buildings. You could be hiding behind a bin in an alley and it would pick you out.

The family walk outside. Dad and I are alone in the entrance. He pulls me into a corner and whispers, *It's a conspiracy. We have to leave the country tonight. We'll go to the harbour, borrow a boat and head for New Zealand.*

Dad is for real. All of a sudden, I realise for sure that the enemy is not out there, but somewhere inside Dad's mind. I also know that we'll die if we go to sea by ourselves. And I do the hardest thing I've ever, ever done.

There's a buzzer on the wall and a microphone next to it. I press it and call for help. Sometimes I wonder if the nurses were already on the way because they get to us so quickly. I can't look at Dad's face as they take him back inside.

Judas! Dad screams at me, and I stay behind howling my eyes out in the corner.

Thought getting this down would help. It hasn't.

Monday July 10th, Prue and Godfrey's

Dad rang tonight. Prue picked the phone up, but I couldn't bring myself to speak to Dad.

School today. Prue and Godfrey made me go. After yesterday, you'd think they would let me skip it for one day. No. They said it would keep my mind off things. Not sure how much they understand about what happened last night, but at least they've kept their mouths shut.

Had my uniform and bag ready. New lunch box, fancy drink container, a pack of felt pens and a pack of coloured pencils in a tartan zip-up thing.

The only way I got through this was to think of you, Mum, as my guardian angel. You were right behind me as I walked into class. Kept pretending all day you'd be outside waiting with all the other mums, just like you used to until Dad wouldn't let you any more and he did it instead.

First bit was murder. When I walked in, the class went pin-drop quiet – then about thirty seconds later the usual noise began and I felt okay.

Mrs Bickerton forced Dean Smith to be my 'buddy' for the day. He said, *Wanna see around?* like he was pretty bored with the idea, especially as it would muck up his plans to play basketball at break. Tagged behind him all recess. Showed me where kids hang out like the stinky toilets, the library, secret places like under the stairwell and behind the sports shed and the different play areas. The whole place is asphalt or concrete. Hardly any grass.

When we were near the basketball court, Dean looked pee-ed off about not playing. *We could both play*, I said. And then I freaked. It's a long time since I even held a basketball.

'Cos I'm tall, the kids passed me the ball to shoot a goal. Missed twice and the groan that went up on my team made me want to throw it all in. This big guy, Ricky Bates, more fat than muscle, called me a dickhead. I said, *You've got it all wrong. You're the hairy Richard.* That got a laugh from the others, but Rick's a bit of a leader. He got back at me by calling me Worm. *Yeah, Worm*, he said. *That about sums up everything you've got.* That brought an even bigger laugh. Everyone in the class is calling me Worm. Don't like it one bit.

Prue's out to prove herself queen of healthy lunches. My lunch box was fairly growing sprouts. Did a swap with two girls, Naomi and Sophie. Scored a chocolate chip muffin and a can of Coke. Naomi and Sophie are on complexion diets 'cos they've each had a pimple in the last month. Sophie could have a hundred pimples and still be cute. She's got curly brown hair and dimples. Dean Smith told me in private that, other than maths which she is hopeless in, Sophie's the brainiest in the grade.

During small group discussion Sophie says to me: *I collect fascinating facts.*

Me: *Like what?*

Sophie: *Like did you know that last year five people in Australia electrocuted themselves on their Christmas tree lights?*

Class seems okay. We're doing Australia Getting Started. In English, did some real Aboriginal poems and in music we sang ballads like *Botany Bay*. For homework have to learn the words to *Advance Australia Fair*. In art learnt how to do watercolour gum trees. All the lessons link up. Mrs Bickerton says it's called an integrated curriculum.

When the class gets noisy, Bickerton yells, *Silence!* and whacks her ruler on the desk. We all jump a mile. That woman would make a good Judge Judy.

Prue and Godfrey asked about my day. Told them how everyone calls me Worm. Godfrey wanted to know what's so bad about that. Had to explain it's lower than dickhead. It's what you get called when you're the world's worst basketball player.

Tried not to think about Dad at school, but couldn't help it. Heart would hammer when I thought about the Judas bit. Tonight asked Prue what Judas means. It's more terrible than I thought. It's a shocking word. Prue and Godfrey say Judas was the friend who dobbed on Jesus and got him killed. A few days later Judas felt so bad that he hanged himself. I am a traitor. But I can't help feeling a bit sorry for Judas.

Tuesday July 11th, Prue and Godfrey's

Dad rang a few minutes back. Still can't face speaking.

Got a recess detention from Judge Judy. She's an evil dictator. It's not fair to keep a new kid in just because he didn't do a bit of homework. Tried to tell her about having to look after the mice.

Me: *I just ran out of time.*

Judge Judy: *As soon as someone says 'just' to me, I know it's an excuse.*

Got home to find Godfrey putting up a basketball ring on a pole in the backyard. He'd bought me a basketball, too. Godfrey showed me how to aim. How to run your eye along the length of your arm like the sights of a rifle. After a while, I started shooting every second or third one through the ring. We were at it for about an hour.

Did my homework. Still practising *Advance Australia Fair.*

Got a bit creative and wrote my own version.

Australians all let us rejoice
For we will soon be free
From horrid ugly Bickerton
We'll chuck her in the sea.
Our school abounds with Bicky's gifts
Of screams and thumps and stares.
We'll all be there to help her shift
And rid us of our cares.
(Repeat last two lines.)

I've just become a father. Or an uncle.

Mervin has given birth to eight babies. I got it wrong. He's a she. The babies look like tiny pink beans. They squeak. Mervin's a good mum, but Merrie is a bit agitated. I suppose it's a strain being a first-time father. Specially if you're called Meredith.

But Prue has dropped a bombshell. Have to see a special social worker at the hospital after school on Saturday. Told Prue it's not me who has the problems. I don't need to see anybody.

Prue says it's Human Services who say I have to go. Maybe they want me to say something about Dad so they can lock him away for ever. Or do they think I'm batty, too, for trying to help Dad escape? Prue said, *It's nothing to do with there being something wrong with you.* Yeah, sure.

Wednesday July 12th, Prue and Godfrey's

Can't believe I'm still alive. Not a good day.

If me and Dean Smith hadn't been asked to take the lunch orders to the office, it would never have happened. But we get to the office and the secretary has gone off somewhere and there on her desk is the microphone the principal uses to speak to the school. I pick it up and start singing my Bickerton song. Dean joins in with the chorus bit about helping her shift and ridding us of our cares. I truly didn't know it was on and that the whole school, grade one to six, was listening to me.

Next thing, the office is like an angry beehive full of adults – Mr Duncan the principal, the vice-principal, the secretary and Judge Judy herself. I get all flustered and think I'm back in court. I start calling her Your Worship.

Dean had to pick up grotty papers for both

breaks. For me it was inside the classroom all recess and lunchtime. It takes a long time to write 'I must strive to be a positive role model for other students and I must use appropriate greetings when speaking to teachers' three hundred times. And when Bickerton saw I'd spelt 'appropriate' with only one 'p', I had to start all over again.

Homework here we go. Maths tonight.

Tragedy. Just looked into my mouse house to see Merrie munching on one of the babies. It was worse than *The X-Files*. I picked Merrie up, threw him into my school bag and zipped it shut until Prue found him another home in a shoebox. What a disgusting cannibal. To think Merrie used to be my favourite. It makes you realise even happy families can have weird secrets.

Dad rang just then. Shook my head when Prue tried to get me to the phone.

Thursday July 13th, Prue and Godfrey's

Bickerton smiled. Let that be recorded. She smiled because my homework was done and I got it all right.

Shot goals with Godfrey this avo. I'm getting them in further and further from the ring.

Mervin seems happier now that Merrie is in solitary

confinement. The seven surviving babies are doing well. Felt sorry for Merrie locked away by himself. Put a cardboard toilet roll in his box. Something for him to explore. He likes it.

Daph rang. She's invited me to stay the weekend after this. I'll meet the twins. Asked Prue and Godfrey. Said *yes* straightaway. They're looking tired.

Dad didn't ring. Goodnight, Dad. Sorry.

Friday July 14th, Prue and Godfrey's

Raining today. The tough ones stayed outside during breaks.

At recess Sophie says: *Naomi wants you to come to the library with us.*

Naomi: *I didn't say that.*

Sophie: *You did so, too.*

Naomi to Sophie: *We both wanted him to come.*

Was glad about Sophie but not about Naomi, so I say: *Well I was going to borrow some books anyway, so we may as well have a game of cards or something.*

Went to the library and borrowed a giant stack of books so that Naomi and Sophie would think that's why I had gone there and then we played

Snap all recess and all lunchtime which was all right except that I reckon Naomi kept her hand on top of mine too long during the snap parts.

Prue drives me over to see this social worker tomorrow. Will try to get out of it.

Dad didn't ring again tonight either.

Will do some reading. Almost added *The Lord of the Rings* to my library pile today, but changed my mind. Couldn't handle it if Frodo doesn't survive.

Saturday July 15th, Prue and Godfrey's

Her name is Felicity and she's all right. She looks friendly enough. Still not sure what she wants from me.

Felicity asked, *What was it like for you when you were with your dad?* Kept my mouth shut. If I say the wrong thing to one of these people, they might keep Dad in hospital for ever.

Then Felicity wanted to know if I felt guilty about what's happened to Dad. Did I think I could have protected him from what's going on. It's like she knew. Didn't mean to open my mouth, but said, *Maybe.* She said, *Lots of people who love someone with a mental illness feel like you do, but they can't rescue them.*

Wanted to ask what she meant, but didn't want to let on how stupid I am.

Felicity said hospital is not a nice place to be, but it's the best way to start to get better. Got tears in my eyes, but looked away so she couldn't see. Was thinking of all the times I knew something was wrong. I wanted to save Dad from it all but I didn't know what to do.

Do your friends know? she asked next.

No, I said, clear and simple. And no way do I ever want my friends to find out. They'll think I'm a freak. But didn't say all this. Was watching Felicity closely in case there was some kind of trap.

Felicity said that it'll be a good day for me when I can talk more freely about what's happened to Dad. That there's nothing to hide. It's just a disease. Easy for her to say. Can you really be so upfront about it? How come when people get angry with each other they chuck insults like *psycho* and *nuts* and *bonkers* and *round-the-twist* and a heap of other words that mean you're insane? You can be crippled, blind, anything but insane. But just as if she'd heard me thinking she said, *I know it's a catastrophe for the families of the mentally ill.* Just looked at her. She wasn't going to get a reaction out of me.

Next it was my turn to ask questions. All I could think to ask was when Dad will be let out. Felicity says that the psychiatrist will decide that. Fat lot of good a social worker is. Dad has been locked away for weeks now.

Felicity says I can see her again or ring her if I want. Might. Might not.

Rang Dad tonight. Felt dead scared waiting while the nurse went to get him. Dad said *hello* in an old sort of way. I said, *Sorry for the other day, Dad.* And Dad said, *I don't blame you for being scared. It's a dangerous world we live in.* And I said, *Yes*, because it's easier just agreeing. Then Dad said, *Love you, son.* And I said, *Me too, Dad.*

Had forgotten that about Dad. He doesn't hold grudges.

9

Sunday July 16th, Prue and Godfrey's

Got stuck into a fantastic book this morning. It's about this kid who is the only survivor of a plane crash up in Canada. Prue and Godfrey left me to it.

Later helped Prue and Godfrey wash their cars. They've both got expensive new cars. They look after them like babies. Then they did this massive house clean-up. Godfrey shares the work right down the middle.

Dad used to do that for Mum – shopping, cooking, vacuuming, everything. He used to call her his princess. Lots of times he'd say to Mum, *You sit there with your mending, princess, and sing to us and your men will clean the place up.*

But there was this other time some restaurant rang to ask Mum to sing on Friday nights. I was right next to the phone. Mum was that excited, but Dad made a fuss about her coming home in the dark. I'm wondering if it was from about then that Mum didn't sing nearly so much.

Visited Dad this avo. When me and Godfrey got to the nurses' station, felt a real fool about the escape night. But the head nurse said, *Hey, Pete* and I said *Hey* back. He didn't act any different towards me. Maybe heaps of people try to escape.

Godfrey said later on, *Your dad looked happy as a sandboy to see you.* Don't know what a sandboy is, but Dad sure did look happy.

Like all the other times, had to keep the conversation going. Told Dad about the mice babies. Dad said, *Safely delivered from the time of trials.* Read Dad my Bickerton poem. Can't tell if he's really listening. He said, *You have the family gift for poetry.* Then told him about Bickerton giving me lines because of this beautiful bit of poetry. Thought I might get a laugh. But Dad said, *Consort not with evil.* He's still not a lot better, but he's safe and looked after.

Mice family doing well. Babies are starting to look like proper mice. Strange how they have to get along without a dad, too. Merrie in solitary. Dad in hospital. Do men find it harder to handle things? Am I going to be like that?

Monday July 17th, Prue and Godfrey's

For sport today the whole class played basketball because of some inter-school comp. this Friday. We're playing Forestburn. No one carried on about the way I played. I'm improving.

Mervin's a good mum. It's cute to watch the babies crawling all over each other and nuzzling up under her for a drink of milk. I've forgiven Merrie. Have been trying to tame him. Prue is letting me bring in Merrie's shoebox for a while each night. I can sit and watch TV or read a book with the box next to me. I let my free hand lie in the box with a bit of birdseed in my palm and I make a whistling sound. If I keep really still, Merrie will walk on to my hand and eat the seed.

Dad rang. He thinks they've made a mistake putting him in hospital. He made a friend today called John. He's an engineer. Dad says John shouldn't be in hospital either. Sure, Dad.

Tuesday July 18th, Prue and Godfrey's

Big news. Was watching the grade six basketball team playing grade five at lunchtime today. Ricky Bates was using his bulk to block the other team wherever he could, when over he goes on his ankle. It takes four kids to carry him off the court. The way he was howling you'd think he'd broken something. It turned out he'd just sprained his ankle. That means he can't play in the big game on Friday. The coach is going to try out me and another kid called Bruce King tomorrow. Told Godfrey when I got home. He got deadly serious with the goal practice. Prue says she'll pack me an energy lunch for tomorrow. Sounds extra disgusting.

Was reading with my hand resting in Merrie's shoebox tonight. He nibbled a few seeds out of my hand and then started walking up my arm.

Rang Dad. Like usual, he told me what he had for dinner. But then real news. Today he went for a walk outside with the nurse and when he got back he had a shower. That shower means a lot. He's forgotten the fear about getting gassed.

Wednesday July 19th, Prue and Godfrey's

Fluked it. Got quite a few goals today. Bruce King knows the rules better, but in the end the coach, Mr Laird, chose me. Bruce will be a reserve. Godfrey says it's not a fluke. He says I've got *aptitude*, and I'm guessing that means I've got the talent.

Other bit of good news is that Dean Smith who's a cool player told the team, *Let's call him Spag, short for spaghetti – tall and thin.*

And the rest of the kids think that's excellent. I like Spag way better than Worm.

Dad rang. He's been thinking about Mum today. He's still saying she must have been forced to leave because there was no note and she always left notes. And it's true. She always left notes. If she went for a walk or next door to Miss Weiss she'd leave a note on the fridge door or on top of a pile of tin cans on the bench so we'd be sure to see it. They'd say things like 'Over at Miss Weiss's', 'Turn the oven off please' or 'Feed the chooks' or 'Give Pete his cough mixture', and there'd be lots and lots of xxxxxxxxxx and ooooooooooo. But the day Dad walked me home from my school round the corner and I was carrying the papier mâché fruit bowl I'd made for Mum, she'd gone off in the car without leaving a note. And there was stuff missing like her make-up and toothbrush and clothes and some photos. Dad and I sat there, waiting, until it was dark. And then the policeman came.

Thursday July 20th, Prue and Godfrey's

Big game tomorrow. Godfrey and I shot goals after school till it was dark.

Friday July 21st, Prue and Godfrey's

We kicked butt in the basketball game against Forestburn. The enemy had some bulky guys and a couple of girls built like trucks. They played pretty dirty, too. Elbows and feet hitting you where it hurts when the ref wasn't looking. But Spaghetti Man didn't let a bit of pain get him down. I'm still not sure of the rules, so I hung around the goal post and did my bit when the ball got to me. Forestburn got eleven goals and we got nineteen. Dean Smith got four of those, Tanya Sorelli got six and I scored nine. Our team went berko. They picked me up on their shoulders and carried me off the court.

Mrs Bickerton said we can have a party on Monday. Dean Smith called out, *Three cheers for Bicky!* We all cheered. Even me.

Rang Dad and told him about the basketball. He said he was proud of me and that he loved me and then he said, *We'll be back together as soon as they realise.*

Prue drives me to the hospital tomorrow. Daph will pick me up from there for my stay.

Have everything packed. I want to show Simone my mouse family. Prue has given me an old cane picnic basket with a hinged lid to put Mervin and her babies in. Merrie has to stay behind.

Saturday July 22nd, Daph and Bill's

Dad had his first visitor other than me today. When Daph and I walked into Dad's room, he looked like it was Christmas. His friend John was sitting there. Dad introduced Daph to him and then John left in a hurry. *We'll finish our talk later*, Dad said to him. Daph and Dad gave each other a big hug. Daph had brought some home-made chocolate chip biscuits and a flask of brewed coffee. Dad rubbed his hands together and said, *You beaut!* We had our morning coffee in the little courtyard near his room.

Dad told Daph about his doctor, his social worker and the nurse who takes him for walks outside the hospital. He didn't ask either of us to get him out of there.

Really liked it when Daph told Dad she admired him for the way he had always done his best for me, and that Mum would think Dad had done a good job with me. Dad's eyes went watery and he said, *I loved her, Daph. I've tried to bring up Pete the way Laura would want me to. And keeping him safe hasn't been easy.*

On the way to Daph and Bill's place in the car, Daph said out of the blue that she was really sorry for not fully understanding Dad's illness. She said, *I'm still trying to figure it out myself. Dr Gibbs, our family doctor, tells me a lot of people with your dad's illness are super-intelligent.*

According to Daph, Dad was a real geek at uni – won prizes and that sort of thing. *He can leave me way behind in a conversation. It's like talking to a dictionary.*

She said she and Bill had known he was disturbed, but they hadn't been able to figure out exactly what was the matter. *He's so intelligent and better educated than Bill and me. He'd have us half-believing what he would tell us.*

Daph says we all have to get rid of this idea of mentally ill people being bad. She said, *Your dad's so generous, I've seen him in mid-winter give away a new coat to a bloke he thought had greater need of it than he did. He reminds me more of Jesus than most of the people I meet at church of a Sunday.*

Well, I know my dad. What Daph says is true.

Daph reckons that if she'd properly understood, she wouldn't have got caught up in the fights and she would have talked Dad into seeing a doctor. *With mental illness, the earlier it gets treated, the better.*

But it was still getting to me how Dad could be mad if he is such a nice intelligent guy. It didn't add up. I said this to Daph. But she said, *Your dad has a real disease like some people get diabetes or arthritis. It's called Skizofrenea.* Not sure how to spell that.

Talking to Daph about this Skiz-whatever-you-call-it disease was like coming up for air after you've been drowning for years and years.

Like the film 'Dr Jekyll and Mr Hyde'? I said. *The guy with the split personality?*

Daph said, *No way. Dr Gibbs says people who think like that have got it badly wrong.*

Daph says the chemicals in the brain get mucked around. You get terrible fears and you might even believe you are hearing or seeing things to do with those fears.

It's beginning to make sense. I'm thinking that life might have been better if I'd been dead certain that the helicopters, planes, black cars, Asio and whatever else weren't after us. I could have helped Dad. We might still be up at McKenzie's Beach.

I wanted to know if the fears will go away.

As long as Michael stays on his medication, he won't be afraid, said Daph. *Don't expect things to be perfect, but they will be a lot better than they have been.*

And then I got thinking about Mum again. Did she understand about Dad? I knew I had to come straight out with the question that has been bugging me since the court case. And this time I wanted a clear answer.

Why did Mum walk out on Dad and me? How could she leave me alone to look after Dad?

Daph went all quiet. My heart was pounding big time.

Then she said, *You can love someone but still find it hellish hard to live with them. Put it out of your mind and just remember that your mum loved you with all her heart.*

That's asking too much. Can't put it out of my mind. And I won't. So I asked why Mum was a bird in a gilded cage. And Daph said she was sorry I'd heard that bit of her row with Dad. Daph said that Dad treated Mum like she might get hurt or broken if she was out of his sight. *She was well looked after, but she was sort of controlled.*

And what Daph said makes sense of the coat hanger night. Mum was a bird bashing its wings against the wire.

But I wouldn't leave my kid to go through all that on his own. No way. I'm jacked off with not knowing things. And just like it bugged Dad, it really, really bugs me that Mum had left no note. How could she leave us so lost and confused?

If she'd left a note, Dad might not have packed us up three days later, straight after the funeral, to go look for her. That's when the wandering began. He couldn't get it into his head that she was dead.

No matter how unhappy I was, I'd be sure to leave a note. It'd be like torturing people on purpose not to leave a note.

Sunday July 23rd, Prue and Godfrey's

The twins rule. There's a boy and a girl. They cry, feed, poo and sometimes sleep. But they do it at different times so there's always something going on. Lorraine doesn't get dressed till about the middle of the afternoon. She drags around the house in her nighty and dressing gown leaking milk all over herself. She calls herself the house cow.

Everyone is on a twins roster. Bill and Daph help Lorraine during the night. Lorraine's husband, Dave, is the night-shift mechanic at a factory so he helps out when he gets home about eight in the morning. Even that wire-haired wild cat Simone is looking pale and tired from being on duty afternoons and evenings. When I showed her Mervin's young family she yawned and said, *Too many babies.*

Glad to be back tonight. Own quiet room. Meals on time.

You spell it Schizophrenia. Oxford Dictionary says, *Mental disease marked by disconnection between thoughts, feelings and actions.* Yeah right. Daph explained it better.

Godfrey and I've made chocolate crackles for tomorrow's class party.

Best bit of day. Godfrey's dad, Neil, came over with a surprise – a mouse castle. Almost a metre square. It's made of wood, but painted to look like stone. Four turrets that the mice can really run up and down. A large medieval hall, a courtyard with space to put mouse exercise equipment. Best of all, a real drawbridge and a portcullis that works. We've got it on the verandah.

Didn't want to hurt Godfrey's feelings about the Mousery. Told him we'd make it like a time-out centre if we get any more fights or bad behaviour. Godfrey says that's a great idea. He's sure we'll get plenty of use for it. We've put Merrie in the Mousery for the moment.

Rang Dad. Told him about Mouse Castle. Think he was listening because he asked, *Early or late Norman architecture?* Don't have a clue. But the question seems normal enough.

Have been thinking about Mum. Need some questions answered. Want to get back to Willow Hill to visit our old neighbour, Miss Weiss.

10

Monday July 24th, Prue and Godfrey's

Bicky kept her word. We had a class party this morning to celebrate the basketball victory. Got out of a double maths.

Was happy to see Prue and Godfrey go to the gym for an hour tonight. Looked up Weiss in the K to Z. There are heaps. But none in Willow Hill. Tried a few anyway. People probably thought I was going to rob them or something because they sounded pretty suspicious, specially when they'd ask me what this Miss Weiss's first name is and who her family are and I couldn't tell them anything.

Wednesday July 26th, Prue and Godfrey's

Stayed over at Dean's last night. His mum picked

us up from school and we had to go to Dean's trumpet lesson before getting to his place. Not sure if my ears will ever recover from having to sit next to Dean practising his trumpet in the car. It made Neville's violin playing seem beautiful. Mrs Smith is one patient lady. There she was driving the car in bumper to bumper afternoon traffic with Dean blasting away in the seat right behind her while she tested Matthew, Dean's six-year-old brother, on his spelling.

Hamburgers and chips for tea. Had a good time on Dean's PlayStation.

When we are in our bunks in Dean's room, I ask where his dad is. He tells me his mum and dad are separated. His dad has a girlfriend and hardly ever has much time for Dean and Matthew. *Dad says it's because of his import business, but that's a load of crap.* Dean misses his dad something terrible.

Dean asks me, *How come you're not living with your mum and dad, Spag?* I tell him Mum is dead and Dad's sick in hospital. When he asks what's the matter with Dad, I say, *They're still trying to find out.* That's sort of true.

Prue says Dean can stay over at our place next week.

Thursday July 27th, Prue and Godfrey's

Basketball practice after school today. Windy and spitting rain, but it didn't stop us. I'm improving my game every day I play. Leg and arm muscles sore tonight.

Was looking in Godfrey's *Street Directory* tonight. Willow Hill is miles away.

Friday July 28th, Prue and Godfrey's

Some girl has left a note on my desk. It says, *Dear Spag, I like the way you don't act like you know you're good-looking.*

Do girls think spaghetti can be good-looking?

Showed Dean note. Told him am wondering which girl has the hots for me.

Dean: *I reckon it's Sophie.*

Me: *I wish! More likely Naomi. She wants to be my partner for everything.*

Dean: *Come to think of it, you're right. She's all over you like a rash.*

Bummer.

Mice going fine. Babies have proper fur now. And they play chasey with each other. Even though they're still suckling, they're beginning to eat food as well. I've started the hand-feeding method with them. I do the whistling thing, too. I want them to come to my call like a dog does.

Rang Dad. He reckons he's been helping John out with his problems. Can mad people help other mad people? Even if they can, Dad's not ready to be let loose in the big bad world. My worst nightmare still is that Dad's never going to get out.

Saturday July 29th, Prue and Godfrey's

Visited Dad. When I got there, he was sitting in the lounge with John and an older lady who was crying. Dad had his arm around her shoulder. *Don't give up. Don't give them the pleasure*, he was saying to her. *Fear not.*

Spent the rest of the visit in Dad's room. He asked whether I'm being looked after properly.

Told him I'm fine. *Take it easy, Dad. I'm fine.* Told him to concentrate on getting better.

Asked him if he remembered Miss Weiss. *Of course. She had a good heart*, says Dad.

Asked what her first name is and how old she'd be. He couldn't remember her name, but he said, *She'd be in her nineties or dead.*

Sunday July 30th, Prue and Godfrey's

Had a nightmare last night. Was young again.

Standing in the doorway of Miss Weiss's good room. The one where she used to sit in her big armchair almost all day long. But she wasn't sitting. She was crashing and banging round the room. Things were tipping over. She was sort of groaning. Woke up feeling yucky. Didn't get rid of the feeling for ages.

Monday July 31st, Prue and Godfrey's

No love notes today, but a 20-cent bag of lollies on the desk.

I reckon it's Naomi. She giggles at everything I say. I hope it's not Naomi. She picks her nose in class.

Then again it could be Tanya Sorelli. She's an Amazon on the basketball court. Amazons used to go to battle with bare breasts. Tanya could do that. The other boys reckon she was the first in the class to show signs of growing boobs.

Maths test tomorrow on long division. Bickerton says we have to get 60% or else. Or what, I'm wondering?

Dad rang. First thing he says is, *Adelaide.* Am thinking Dad's getting worse again. *No one's heading for Adelaide, Dad. You take it easy.* But Dad says, *Her name is Adelaide.*

Tuesday August 1st, Prue and Godfrey's

Failed maths test. Had to stay in at lunchtime and do extra maths. In silence.

Was raining so didn't mind too much. Had some company, anyway. Six of us. Me, Dean, Frank Hall, Tony Cini, Tanya and Sophie. We kept passing notes right under Bickerton's nose while she munched on her lunch and marked our books.

Was quite enjoying it all. Was just writing back to the others how I thought we should call ourselves the V.M.C. (Vegie Maths Club) when Bicky looks up and starts sweeping the room with her metal detector eyes. I stuff the note in my pocket. Dean distracts her with, *You can't divide 597 by 4331, Miss.* And she cracks it with Dean and says, *Try it the other way round, Einstein.*

Adelaide. What a name to call a kid. No wonder Miss Weiss was single and bald.

Probably was Mum's only friend in the street, though.

Wednesday August 2nd, Prue and Godfrey's

Dean's here. Mice babies growing so fast I swear you can see it happening. Worried about a couple of them who are looking quite a lot bigger than the rest. According to my latest research, male mice can breed when they're five to six weeks old. Females can get pregnant when they're twelve weeks. I think we're safe, but Godfrey says maybe we should look into family planning.

Dad still pretty much the same.

Thursday August 3rd, Prue and Godfrey's

Dean came over last night. Shot goals out the back and then did our homework together. Yesterday Bickerton gave the V.M.C. ten long divisions. Godfrey helped us with them. Showed us some neat short cuts. First time ever, Dean and I think we've got the hang of it. Dean said, *Godfrey's cool.* Still know it should be Dad helping Dean and me with our maths. Wish someone would say my dad's cool.

Begged Prue not to give us anything healthy for tea. Told her if she did, Dean wouldn't ever, ever want to visit again. *Oh dear*, she said, *I was planning rice patties and steamed spinach.* Then she laughed and landed me a pretend punch on the shoulder. Didn't let me down. She made chicken nuggets and chips followed by fruit salad with ice cream instead of yoghurt. Mum used to make chocolate mousse for special times.

Got Adelaide Weiss on my mind. Remembered

something else today. Mum used to have conversation lessons with Miss Weiss in French or German or something. It used to bug me that Mum could speak in this secret code and leave me out of things.

Friday August 4th, Prue and Godfrey's

Good of Dean to lend me the money and not push with the questions. Everything's ready.

I'm going to find Miss Weiss.

11

Sunday August 6th, Prue and Godfrey's

Grounded. Couldn't give a rat's arse.

Because the police were waiting for me when I got back last night, I've missed writing in this for yesterday. Anyway I was stuffed.

Prue and Godfrey went off their brains when I walked in at ten p.m. Note didn't work. Prue and Godfrey rang Dean's mum. Dean's probably copping it, too. Have some explaining to do to Dean.

Prue and Godfrey think they've got a delinquent on their hands. That's what Godfrey said, *Behaving like a delinquent.* He got really stirred up 'cos I didn't seem to care. Even the two cops couldn't wreck my day. Acted like I was listening to their telling me off, but wasn't.

Yesterday was some day. I go over and over it like a film in my head. Me sneaking out while it's still dark and misty. Leaving the note on the kitchen bench at Prue and Godfrey's saying Dean and I've gone to the footie. Was dressed for it, too – coat with the collar turned up, Tiger's beanie. Didn't strike me that freezing cold dawn is a pretty dumb time to go to the footie. The point is, I'd done the right thing and left the note. I'd never not leave a note.

Was standing on Flinders St Station, central Melbourne, feeling pretty pleased with myself. Had to walk for ages and then catch a bus to get there. Was looking up at all the clocks and destinations and could see Willow Hill almost at the end of the Northern line. An hour and a half later I was standing in Willow Hill main street – a country store with a 'Post Office' sign in the window next to some potatoes and big orange pumpkins. There's also a mini-mart supermarket, a cafe, a community hall and two white painted churches, one each side of the street staring straight at each other.

It felt like I'd never been there before. And that's about the truth of it, because Dad stopped Mum and me going to the shops pretty early on. But then I saw the park with its Lest We Forget memorial and the five or six skinny gum trees that make it look like a desert even in winter. But a smaller desert than I remember. Over the far side you could see the school fence.

Didn't have a clue what the name of our old street is, but was counting on remembering my way home from school. Next thing, I was standing in front of the main school building. It's got 1916 on the archway over the front porch. I watched the five- and six-year-old ghost of myself running down the front steps and out to Mum or Dad.

I started the walk home. Past the house where the lady grew roses. Turned right at the corner. Went quickly past the stinky chicken farm. Turned left. Could see our little yellow place from the corner. Thought maybe Dad was right. Maybe Mum's not dead. Maybe she was just waiting there for us. But I was standing at the gate and there were all these weeds in the garden where Mum grew herbs and old-fashioned flowers and then this big bloke with tats walked out the door and said, *What y'starin' at?*

This used to be my place, I said.
Yeah? Well it's not now.

It was starting to rain. Not heavy. Just drizzle. I walked next door to Miss Weiss's. Her name *WEISS* was still on the metal letter box. The front yard was even more of a cactus jungle than I remembered. When I got to the door, I pressed the bell and waited. Miss Weiss always took a long time to let you in because of her bad sight. So I was waiting, but the waiting took for ever. I pressed the bell again.

You wanting the old lady?

I really did jump. There was this woman, maybe about fiftyish, standing at the other bordering fence. She was smiling.

Yes. I used to live in the yellow house. Six years ago.

We've only been here about a year, love. But they tell me the old dear got crook a couple of months before we came and was moved to the Bluebird nursing home.

Is she still alive? Was thinking to myself that she just had to be alive.

Well, I wouldn't know. But it's a good sign that the house isn't on the market yet.

I headed back to Willow Hill station. Miss Weiss's new neighbour had told me the nursing home was two stops back towards the city and I'd see it from the trainline. It was a long wait for a train, so it was midday and raining hard by the time I got to the front door of the Bluebird home.

It was like being back at Dad's hospital. You have to push a buzzer and only a nurse can open the door because the hallway is lined with old people in wheelchairs or old people just moving around like sleepwalkers. One of the sleepwalkers, a little lady in a pink dressing gown, says to me, *Will you take me home, dear? I've lost my way.* You can tell pretty quickly that most of these fossils can't remember anything except that they want to go home.

I'm thinking, is this why Miss Weiss is here? Has she forgotten everything, including my mum?

The nurse at reception wants to know if I'm 'family'. I say, *No. But Aunty Adelaide was like a grandma to me when I was little.*

The 'Aunty Adelaide' is a bit of a whopper, but it does the trick.

The nurse tells me that Miss Weiss came in to recover from a broken hip, but then got heart trouble and then – worst news of all – *began to lose it. She often just talks to herself in German. And you'd better prepare yourself. Her sight is a lot worse and she's also very deaf now.*

So I'm taken to Miss Weiss's room. It's like the room Dad and I had that time in Flinder's Street. One little window looks directly at a brick wall. No sun. No nothing. But then, Miss Weiss is blind. So maybe she doesn't care.

I can see a hump sitting in a reclining armchair, little swollen legs propped up. A hump with a ventolin mask over the face. But it's Miss Weiss because you can see the pink, bald head with even fewer wisps of white hair than six years ago. Only difference now is there are spiky white hairs growing on her chin.

You have a visitor, Del! the nurse shouts into Miss Weiss's good ear. I'm thinking no one ever called Miss Weiss Del. But when you get to a place like this, they can call you anything they want. The nurse takes the mask off. Miss Weiss's blind eyes move around trying to see.

It's Pete from next door, I say into the good ear.

Josef? says Miss Weiss. And then she's gabbling away in German and all I think I can hear is something like, *zurück kehren*. And then she says in English, *My little brother!*

See, says the nurse. *You probably won't get a word of sense out of her.* I feel like telling the nurse to piss off, but she walks out of the room anyway.

I'm Laura's boy, Miss Weiss.

Laura! Laura! And the tears just roll down Miss Weiss's face. I never knew you'd still have tears after you've gone blind. She puts her hands out and holds my face.

Miss Weiss pulls my head towards her and whispers, *Liebling, I have the package. But I am so, so shocked when Laura is killed that I can't find it. I get all muddled up. I spend days looking. I am calling to the Lord to help my eyes find it. And three days later I do, but your father is gone. And I am waiting all these years.*

Miss Weiss, please. What package?

Look for a tin box. Over there in the cupboard. Look, little Peter, before they come back.

And I go to the cupboard and boy do I look. I'm chucking nighties and knickers around like ladies do in a sale. And it's there at the back of a drawer. A small grey tin box like you'd keep money in.

I've got the box, Miss Weiss, I say, and I kiss her on her white cheek.

Yah, it is good, she smiles. Then she shuts her blind eyes.

I'd love to know more about my mum, Miss Weiss.

Kirschtorte, Josef?

And I know Miss Weiss has left me.

Then I hear a rattling sound. It's the lunch lady pushing her trolley into the room. I'm standing there with the tin box in my hands and the room is a mess. Things don't look good.

You bloody little thief! the lunch lady screams. *Help!*

No way to explain. I dive past her and knock plates and cutlery to the ground. It makes a shocking noise. I run down the hall, past the wheelchairs and the walking dead. A man with his little daughter is just going out the front door. I push past and through. The lady in the pink dressing gown calls out, *Take me with you, boy!*

Personally, I don't see it as pure luck; but the fact is, by the time I've done the fastest run of my life to the station, a train is just ready to head for the city. I jump on, grab a corner seat in the carriage and the train pulls out. I look across to the Bluebird home. A male nurse is jogging towards the station.

I have the carriage to myself. That's when I open the box. There's a thick envelope inside. On the front, written in biro, is: *For Michael and Peter. Per Kind Favour of Miss A. Weiss.*

No mistake about it, this is for Dad and me. Mum touched this envelope and wrote on it and meant it for us. She's speaking to us from the dead. It's like a shipwrecked sailor stuck on an island has put a message in a bottle and chucked it into the ocean and years later the bottle is found but the messenger is dead.

Maybe someone else would rip into the envelope really fast. Not me. My mum sealed this envelope and I try to picture her doing it, licking the glue, pressing the bit that sticks, maybe sighing and holding it to her heart. I slowly, slowly tear it open like I'm entering somewhere sacred.

Inside are two other envelopes and what feels like

a book wrapped in a plastic bag. The first envelope has *Michael* written on it. I'd make sure Dad got this straightaway. No going back to Prue and Godfrey's until Mum's wishes have been respected. The second letter says *Pete* and I open this one.

December 10th

My Dearest Peter,

Don't be sad because I'm not with you at home. It's only for a little while. You know Mummy has been crying a lot lately. It's because I need a holiday and time to plan our lives. Daddy is always worrying about things and I so much want us all to be happy.

I'm going to find a pretty place to stay for a couple of weeks.

Do you remember us reading 'Winnie the Pooh'? Well just like Pooh, your mum needs to go on a fast Thinking Walk. I want to find a Thoughtful Spot and think some big thoughts. And whatever my Thinking will be, you, my precious one, will be part of the very breath I breathe. Much of my Thinking will be about how to plan for you to grow up into the best sort of person you can be.

I wish so many good things for you. I wish for you to have a good education, lots and lots of friends, and happy parents. I'm sure you wish this, too.

Now Daddy will probably get upset when he

reads his letter. He always thinks you and I have to be near home to be safe. But I'm telling you that everything is okay and it's going to get better. As soon as I arrive at the pretty holiday place, I will ring you.

Say your prayers each night. Help Dad with the dishes. Water my flowers if they look thirsty. Keep an eye on Miss Weiss.

Just to keep you company, I've made up a little album of favourite photos for you to keep by the bed.

I love you until for ever,

Mummy   xxxxxxxxxx ooooooooooo

The book in the plastic bag turns out to be a small photo album. There's me, Dad and Mum smiling out of the photos. My beautiful, beautiful Mum. Mum with flowers in her hair on her wedding day. Mum and Dad bathing me as a baby. Mum pulling a silly face right up next to the camera. Mum standing on Dad's shoulders like a circus act. Mum, Dad, me and my birthday cake (Miss Weiss's Kirschtorte) on my sixth birthday – Mum is kissing me. And I pick that one up and lean it against my cheek so that Mum can kiss me again.

Monday August 7th, Prue and Godfrey's

Spent lunchtime under the stairwell sitting on

milk crates telling Dean *everything* – childhood, Mum dying, the wandering round the Eastern states, McKenzie's Beach and my mate Vic, Melbourne life, Heritage Hotel up in the hills, capture, court, foster care, hospital and now Miss Weiss.

Dean didn't budge while I talked. At the end he said, so quiet I almost didn't hear, *Shit.*

Was thinking about Mum saying she wants me to be the best person I can be. Feel a bit bad about leaving Prue and Godfrey out of things. They've been trying their hardest. When I got home from school, I said sorry for Saturday and for not explaining yesterday. Told them about Miss Weiss and Mum. They gave me a hug and I let them.

Keep reading Mum's letter over and over again. Will know it by heart soon.

Didn't ever think a face could glow till I saw Dad holding his letter last night. *She loved me. If we had counselling she was going to come back to work it out*, he said. *The only thing stopping her coming back was that she died, you know.* Dad was still hanging on to that bit of paper as I left the room. Reckon he probably slept with it.

Dad rang. Seems calmer.

Tuesday August 8th, Prue and Godfrey's

Had to write stories in pairs today. Our topic is 'An early settler's journal'.

Bickerton wouldn't let us choose our writing partners. Dean has to sit with Naomi. Frank is with Tanya and so on. I have to sit with Sophie.

I get all inspired when I remember doing exactly this with Vic in our lessons with Dad. We wrote 'Black Knight's Revenge'. Then Vic and I decided to make a video of it. Anna is a nun who gets stabbed in the gizzards by a white knight who has gone bad – that's Marco. The black knight (Dad) who has loved the nun since she was a kid fights the white knight. Dad and Marco have this amazing sword fight on the De Lucias' carport roof. It's lucky that Marco only breaks a big toe when he falls off. Vic gets right up close with the camera while Marco is rolling round on the ground. That's the best bit of the film, 'cos Marco is the one who has to die, anyway.

I tell Sophie all about 'Black Knight's Revenge' and hint we could sort of do the same thing. Just change it enough to be Australian. But Sophie can't see what a brilliant idea it is. So she starts giving me her idea of a good story and I have to write it down. At least we've agreed that I'll get a go at being author halfway. There I am writing away.

Her part of the story is pretty soppy. Think she got a lot of it off some TV show.

There's this Irish convict girl called Morag (what a name) who has been sent to Australia for stealing a loaf of bread. The boat pulls into Sydney and a whole lot of lonely bushmen are at the wharf hoping to choose a wife. They all want Morag because she's such a good looker. But Morag won't have any of them because they don't shave and they're not good-looking enough. Instead, Morag chooses to be a servant-girl for this tall, dark, handsome stranger who shaves and dresses as cool as can be.

The stranger is an English lord who had got sick of English winters and wanted to be nice and warm for a change. Lord George has got all these convicts to build him this stone mansion.

It turns out that Morag is the daughter of a very poor Irish lord and lady who had died during the potato famine. She's ashamed of what's happened to her so she doesn't tell Lord George, but he finds out because he has noticed Morag's hands are all white and smooth and she can play the piano really well and sings like an angel.

Morag and George were just getting to the point

where they were falling in love when I felt the story needed some action. Besides, my writing hand was getting tired.

Sophie takes over with the writing and I become the ideas man. I send Lord George off on horseback to do some droving. Morag and George need a break from each other. Anyway, I secretly plan to kill off Lord George.

First I send in some Aborigines who spear George. Sophie gets upset. *You have to let Morag ride out to George. She wants to nurse him.* I give in, but I won't let them kiss. *If you're in that much pain, you wouldn't want to kiss.* Then I decide to send in some bushrangers who are going to ransack George's mansion and shoot George.

Sophie gets all unreasonable, so we argue until recess.

Wednesday August 9th, Prue and Godfrey's

What a day. Walk into class this morning with my hands jammed in my jacket pockets to keep them warm. Bickerton wants us to do a classroom clean-up, so I decide to do a personal spring clean as well.

Start on my pockets:
Lolly wrappers
Fake Pokemon card Tony Sorelli made on his computer
Five cents
Note the V.M.C. were passing during maths detention
Love note left on my desk

Just about to chuck all this in the bin when I get a shock.

Uncrumple the love note. Swirly artistic handwriting.

Look again at note us maths morons wrote in detention. One message out of six has swirly, artistic handwriting.

Race to work tub and pull out yesterday's early settler story. The bit of the story Sophie wrote has swirly artistic handwriting.

Sophie likes me.

Thursday August 10th, Prue and Godfrey's

Like Sophie and everything, but didn't know what to say to her. Found it hard even looking at her.

Godfrey's mum and dad came over tonight. Neil's made this excellent mouse mirror maze that fits into the castle courtyard. *It will increase their intelligence*, he said. They definitely could do with that.

Two weeks left till holidays.

Saturday August 12th, Prue and Godfrey's

Prue and I carried my mouse castle in to show Dad today. Only got as far as the front desk before the nursing staff stopped us. They wanted a look. In the end we had the shrink, the ward nurses, a whole lot of patients and some visitors including this teenage kid called Troy inspecting the castle. Everyone thinks it's the best idea they've ever seen.

The mouse stories that went around were awesome. There's this patient called Eric who used to be a farmer and he had these unbelievable mouse plagues every couple of years. *1976 there were that many of the buggers, they even ate me wife's wedding dress.* The things Eric used to do to the mice he caught. Gross.

Might have made my first sale today. Troy wants to buy some mice. He's been visiting his mum a couple of times a week. Didn't ask what's up with her. Guess he gets as pissed off as I do by questions. Anyhow, we're hoping I could hand across the mice when we're at the hospital next weekend. Troy's dad says he wants to think about it first. Troy and I have swapped phone numbers.

Can't remember when Dad last went on about this Asio crap. Cross my fingers and all that, looks like his mind's clearing.

Sunday August 13th, Prue and Godfrey's

Daph called by with Simone today. *Punch or a story?* Simone says, running at me. *How about basketball, instead?* I say. She looks a bit surprised, but says, *Okay.* Taught her to shoot goals. She's halfway reasonable.

Merrie has been released into the castle. Prue says he's on a good behaviour bond, which is what you get if the judge thinks you'll try hard not to muck up. Merrie's made no more attacks on his children. Anyway, they're big enough to look after themselves.

Monday August 14th, Prue and Godfrey's

Have to do speeches on Wednesday. We have to talk about anything we're interested in. And we have to bring props.

Godfrey brought home a drip water feeder and two plastic Ferris wheels that he got at some pet shop. One Ferris wheel is for Merrie. I think he's marked it out as his territory – wee-ed on it or something. The other mice don't dare go near it. The second ferris wheel is for the rest of the family. Have kept up with their training most nights.

Tuesday August 15th, Prue and Godfrey's

Troy rang tonight. His dad says no to mice. Bummer. Wouldn't recommend mice breeding as a way to get rich.

Troy and I got talking about our parents and their illnesses. Troy said, *It's like when I knock on the door, there's no one home.*

Or like an empty room? I said.

Same dif, he said.

Suppose it doesn't matter what the illness is. If it gets bad enough, you still end up losing your parent.

Troy wants to know what I'm doing these holidays. Told him not that much. Probably the shire holiday programme. Maybe a night at Daph and Bill's. Troy says there's this camp being run by Felicity's boss from the hospital. It's for kids like him and me. It's out in the bush and there's a ropes course and lots of cool stuff like that. And the food is great. Troy's been to three already. Started two years ago when he was twelve. Says by being with other kids who have parents with problems you feel less of a freak. You handle things better. He reckons I should go.

Wednesday August 16th, Prue and Godfrey's

Speeches today. Interesting to hear the different things the other kids are into.

Tanya Sorelli collects signatures. Her most famous ones are from Cathy Freeman, Olivia Newton-John and some old Gallipoli bloke who died a couple of days after signing her book.

Ricky Bates and his dad have a model train set. A whole room for it. Sounds like his dad gets to play with it more than Ricky does, though.

Naomi does tap dancing. She gave us a demo. No comment.

As well as fascinating facts, Sophie collects stamps. Her great-uncle gave her his stamp album which he started in 1932 and Sophie is keeping it going.

Dean Smith played his trumpet. Just about everyone stuck their fingers in their ears, but at the end they clapped and cheered.

Godfrey drove my mouse castle to school and helped carry it into class for me. It was a hit. Mouse Castle is a happy and busy home. Anywhere you look there is something going on.

Mice on the Ferris wheel or exploring the mirror maze. Mice pattering up and down the towers. Other mice with their quivering, whiskery noses and beady eyes looking out at us through the portcullis. It was a sensation. Everyone wants a mouse. Bicky says first they have to bring a permission letter from home.

Rang Dad. He was stoked that Mouse Castle went down well with the class.

Thursday August 17th, Prue and Godfrey's

None of the class brought a mouse permission letter. But Sophie came up with a great idea. *Mum says she doesn't mind if I take a mouse home for a couple of nights. You know, sort of borrow it.* The other kids think they could do that, too. Even Bicky got excited. She's going to set up a mouse library.

Friday August 18th, Prue and Godfrey's

Mouse library is up and running. Brought my three biggest babies to school in a shoebox. Bicky stored it in her filing cabinet and at the end of school she lent the mice out in margarine containers with air-holes in the lids. I had to type out care instructions on the computer and each borrower got a copy. Bicky wrote the date and the borrowers' names down on a card. Sophie, Dean and Naomi have mice for the weekend, and there are twelve other kids on a waiting list.

Saturday August 19th, Prue and Godfrey's

Visited Dad today. Godfrey said he had a gut feeling it was the right time to meet Dad.

We found him sitting on his bed all dressed up. He looked smart. It was the first time Dad had seen Godfrey, but he knew who he was. Dad stood and shook Godfrey's hand.

Thank you for looking after my boy, he said.

Thank you for lending him to us. You've done a fine job with him. He's welcome to stay with us until you're ready to be together.

The doctor says I'll be out in my own flat before the month's up.

We've had a phone call, too. Human Services say that all going well Pete will be back with you for Christmas. I saved the news so I could tell you both at the same time, said Godfrey, smiling.

I was proud of both those men. They were magnificent.

Dad told us he was allowed to go for a walk outside the hospital without any supervision. It was an amazing feeling walking out the hospital doors. Almost scary. I was wondering if Dad could handle it. Godfrey went and waited in the car while Dad and I headed for a park across the road. I was a boy doing something ordinary with his dad. We stood for a while under some giant old trees and looked at a man chucking a stick for his dog.

A boy should have a dog, said Dad.

I'd like a dog, I said, *but this boy only needs his dad.*

Dad squeezed my shoulder. *This boy has got his dad*, he said.

Suddenly a helicopter roared towards us across the city. Dad stopped still. The helicopter hovered low over the park. Dad pulled me closer and squinted up into the sky. We'd been through all this lots of times. A snooping helicopter always made Dad smell danger. What if Dad wanted us to make a run for it? Would I run, too? How many years before I'd see Daph, Bill and the family again? And the twins growing up – and all my new friends – and Prue and Godfrey, Neil and Allison – and the kids at school?

I knew in my heart I'd have no choice. If the medication hadn't got rid of the fear and Dad felt he had to run, I'd go with him. Thanks for the healthy food and all the sport, Prue and Godfrey. You did your best with me. Neil and Allison, you were great step-grandparents. Goodbye, Dean. Think of me sometimes when you're shooting goals. And goodbye, Sophie. I never told you, but I like you, too. Please look after my mice.

Dad's voice cut through the goodbyes in my head. I looked up as he spoke. He was smiling.

That's a Channel Seven news helicopter, he said, casual as anything. *I wonder what's going on?*

I just hugged him.

C/O Prue and Godfrey COWPER
10 Ascot Ave
Berringarra   3693

October 27th 2000

Dear Vic,

How's things? Lots to tell you.
Dad said to ask if it's okay for us
to come and stay a week or two
this Christmas. I want to climb
the cliff again and see the eagles.

All the best,
Pete

VICTOR DE LUCIA
P.O. BOX 15
MCKENZIE'S BEACH
N.S.W. 2955

Acknowledgements

My heartfelt thanks to the following people:

Angel Marcos Ojeda who is my angel; Drs Christopher and Leonie Kirkby for wisdom, information and encouragement; Rose Cuff of CHAMPS, Victoria, for enthusiastic support; Nicky Lane who gave me a survivor's tour of Melbourne; my students at school for their interest and suggestions; Jackie Pinkster and Esther O'Rourke-de-Graaf for valuable insights; my family (both immediate and extended) for practical assistance and for their faith in me over a very long time; copy-editor Georgia Murray who has shown an instinctive feel for what I was trying to achieve and did far more than just fix up my mistakes; and finally, and of ultimate importance, my editor – Ele Fountain – who did a great deal of 'hand holding' as she patiently led me through the editorial process. Ele Fountain shared the vision and believed in the importance of the story, and for this I will be for ever grateful.

Elizabeth Fensham

Elizabeth Fensham was born in Sydney, Australia, and raised in an Anglican boys' boarding school. Her father, who was the headmaster, was a wonderful spinner of yarns and wrote when he had the time. From an early age, she saw herself as a writer. Her storytelling skills were honed in her teens when she would distract the primary school boarders from homesickness with serialised, blood-curdling bedtime stories.

Elizabeth has been teaching for the last fifteen years in a tiny school in the hills where she lives. She is the head of the English department by virtue of the fact that she is the only one in the English department. She has been writing in earnest for seventeen years, and she has two sons. The older one (25 years old) is an artist. The younger (16 years old) has been a magician since he was 9 years old.

Elizabeth writes:

'I have known a number of children who have family members suffering from schizophrenia. Information booklets were not enough to ease their pain and bewilderment. I searched the library shelves for a fiction novel that might both entertain and inform, but could find nothing. With *Helicopter Man* I have attempted to fill the gap.'

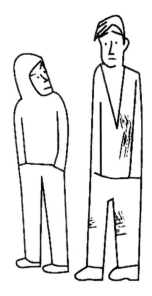

Also from Bloomsbury

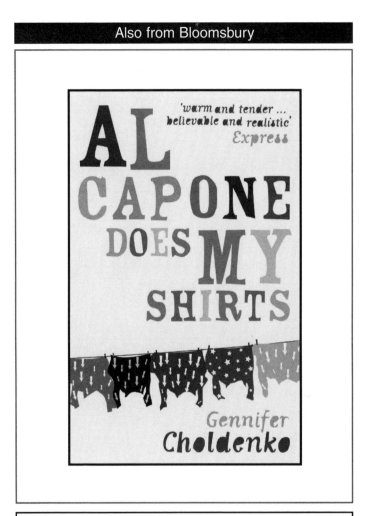

To order from Bookpost PO Box 29 Douglas Isle of Man IM99 1BQ www.bookpost.co.uk
email: bookshop@enterprise.net fax: 01624 837033 tel: 01624 836000

BLOOMSBURY

www.bloomsbury.com

Also from Bloomsbury

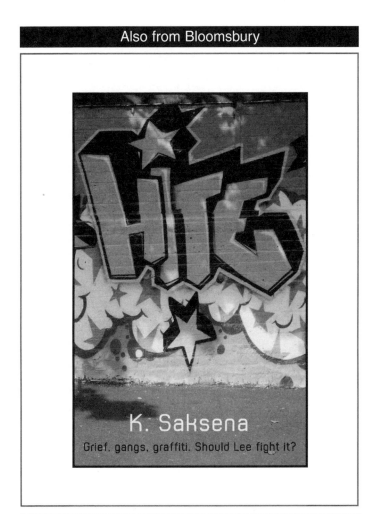

To order from Bookpost PO Box 29 Douglas Isle of Man IM99 1BQ www.bookpost.co.uk
email: bookshop@enterprise.net fax: 01624 837033 tel: 01624 836000

BLOOMSBURY

www.bloomsbury.com